SCARY STORIES FOR STORMY NIGHTS #7

Mark Kehl

ROXBURY PARK

LOWELL HOUSE JUVENILE

LOS ANGELES

NTC/Contemporary Publishing Group

Published by Lowell House
A division of NTC/Contemporary Publishing Group, Inc.
4255 West Touhy Avenue, Lincolnwood (Chicago), Illinois 60646-1975
U.S.A.

Lowell House books can be purchased at special discounts when
ordered in bulk for premiums and special sales. Contact Department CS
at the following address:
NTC/Contemporary Publishing Group
4255 West Touhy Avenue
Lincolnwood, IL 60646-1975
1-800-323-4900

ISBN: 1-56565-965-1
Library of Congress Catalog Card Number: 98-66685

Roxbury Park is a division of NTC/Contemporary Publishing Group,
Inc.

Managing Director and Publisher: Jack Artenstein
Editor in Chief, Roxbury Park Books: Michael Artenstein
Director of Publishing Services: Rena Copperman
Editorial Assistant: Nicole Monastirsky
Interior Designer: Treesha Runnells

Printed and bound in the United States of America
10 9 8 7 6 5 4 3 2

CONTENTS

THE SINKHOLE

———•—— ⊱⬦⬨⬩⬦⬨⬩⬦ ——•———

IT WAS TONY'S FAULT THEY MISSED THE SCHOOL BUS.

Crystal and the others were waiting for the bus at the bottom of the hill, where Raven Hill Court met the main road. Of the seven families that lived on Raven Hill Court, five had children that went to Lexington Middle School, including Crystal. The bus picked them all up at the bottom of the hill.

Crystal's family had lived there only since the summer, but over the first few months of school she had gotten to know the others at the bus stop well. Fred was leaning against the stop sign, dozing, as usual; he always stayed up too late watching TV and was a zombie until lunchtime. Sheryl and Lisa, two grades lower than Crystal, had their lunch boxes open, swapping cookies—peanut butter for chocolate chip.

The other two kids at the stop, Tony and his younger brother Stevie, weren't there yet. Lots of mornings the bus driver had to honk and honk until they came running down the hill, shoes untied and lunch sacks clamped in their teeth as they struggled into their jackets. This was fine with Crystal. The less time she spent around Tony the better.

She thought he liked her, which was kind of nice, but he showed it by sneaking snakes into her book bag and frogs into her lunch. That she could definitely do without.

Still, when Stevie came running out of the woods on the other side of the road with bad news about his brother, she was as concerned as the others.

"Help!" Stevie called as he staggered to the middle of the road. "Tony's hurt!"

He ran back into the trees, and the others rushed to follow. Beyond where the side of the hill had been leveled for the road, the hillside began to slope down again, dropping into a ravine. Crystal could hear the creek burbling at the bottom. The recent rain had also made the narrow trail that wound down the hillside muddy. Crystal and the others descended it in single file, often slipping in the mud and falling into each other, grabbing saplings on either side to steady themselves.

"What happened to Tony?" Crystal called ahead, fretting about her white shoes getting all muddy and then feeling bad for worrying about her shoes when Tony was hurt.

Stevie answered, but over the sounds of everyone sliding down the trail all she caught was ". . . man with a knife." Crystal felt an icy tingle down her back and started to peer into the surrounding trees. The leaves had turned shades of orange and brown and many had fallen, but enough remained on the branches so that she couldn't see more than 20 feet or so in any direction. And with all the noise the children were making, they would never hear a man sneaking up on them until it was too late.

They reached the bottom of the trail. The creek was high, and its muddy water looked like chocolate milk, frothing around fallen trees jammed between its banks.

Fred came last. Still half asleep, he piled into Crystal and Sheryl, and all three nearly tumbled into the muddy water.

"Look out!" Crystal cried, arms waving to catch her balance at the creek's edge.

Stevie was already rushing away along the bank of the creek, and the others hurried after him.

"How much farther is it?" Lisa whined. Crystal couldn't blame her. All of their shoes were coated with mud, and muddy streaks showed on their clothes, hands, and faces from various slippery mishaps.

Stevie didn't answer, but he didn't have to. They suddenly emerged into a small clearing where Tony lay in a bed of delicate wild ferns. He was on his back with his arms flung out and would have looked as if he were sleeping if not for the black hilt of an enormous knife sticking out of his chest.

"Oh, no!" Crystal cried.

The others circled around Tony in solemn silence, as if they were afraid of waking him.

"We have to . . . do something," Crystal said, but she wasn't sure what.

"Is he dead?" Fred asked, his whisper barely loud enough to be heard over the noise of the creek.

"We have to get him to a hospital," Sheryl said.

"I don't think we should move him," Lisa countered. "They say that on doctor shows on TV."

"We need to get help," Crystal said. "Fred, you're the fastest. Go back up to Lisa's house—it's the closest—and tell her mom to call an ambulance."

"Why not the police?" Fred protested. "He looks dead. If he's dead, we don't need an ambulance. We need the police to catch the guy who did it."

"He may not be dead," Crystal insisted, "so we need an ambulance just in case."

Fred studied Tony skeptically. "He sure looks dead. Someone should check his neck for a pulse."

"That's a good idea," Lisa said, obviously impressed. "That's what they do on TV."

Fred looked smug, but Crystal was in his science class and knew he had just learned about the circulatory system and how to take a pulse a few weeks ago, just as she had.

"So take his pulse," she said.

Fred crossed his arms over his chest and shook his head. "No way. I'm not touching a dead person."

"But we don't know he's dead," she said.

He shrugged. "So you check."

The others all looked at Crystal. She didn't much want to touch a dead person either, but somebody had to do it, and they were wasting time.

"Fine," she said. "I will."

She stepped closer to Tony's still body. The ferns tickled her ankles as she moved through them. When she was just close enough to reach out and touch him, she crouched. She held out two fingers toward his neck, moving slowly and carefully. The others pressed in a little closer, shifting around so they could see. Her fingertips touched his skin.

Tony sat straight up and screamed at the top of his lungs. Crystal leaped away, almost slipping on the ferns, shrieking even louder than Tony. Her heart was beating so hard she thought it was going to burst out of her chest.

Tony fell back into the ferns, curling up with laughter. Fred and Stevie were watching her and laughing too. The other girls looked stunned, but their looks of shock were changing to disgust as they realized they had been tricked.

"That wasn't funny, Tony," Crystal snapped.

"You are *soooo* wrong," Tony gasped before surrendering to another laughing fit.

Stevie was doing his impression of Crystal's reaction to Tony's sitting up for Fred's amusement. Crystal was about to tell them what a bunch of immature jerks they were when a familiar sound came over the sound of the creek.

"Listen!" she commanded.

Even the giggling boys quieted for a moment, and they all heard it: the distant honking of the school bus's horn. All five kids starting running at the same time, Tony pulling the fake knife out of his shirt as he brought up the rear. They followed the creek bank back to the bottom of the trail and then started to struggle back up. The slick mud made climbing treacherous, and they had to rely on saplings to pull themselves upward. The honking horn spurred them onward, but when they were about halfway up it stopped.

"Now look what you did," Crystal snapped over her shoulder at Tony. "You made us miss the bus."

"Nah," Tony said. "Mr. Black'll wait for us. He waits longer than this for me and Stevie all the time."

Crystal saved her breath for struggling back up the trail, but she was thinking, *Yeah, but who knows how long he was up there waiting? He could have been honking for a while before I heard him.*

It turned out she was right. When the group of tired and muddy kids stumbled out of the woods, the road was empty. The school bus had gone on without them.

"This is just great," Crystal said angrily.

Stevie looked frightened. "If Dad finds out why we missed the bus," he said to Tony, "we're in for it."

"Look," Tony said, holding up his arms, "there's no problem here. We can walk."

"I don't know," Sheryl said. "It's pretty far. And we'll be late."

"Not to worry," Tony assured her. "It's only far if you stay on the road. I know a shortcut that will get us there before the second bell rings. Nobody's going to be late."

He started walking down the road in the direction of the school. The others looked at one another, unwilling to trust him but lacking any other ideas. Finally, Crystal sighed and started to follow Tony. The others came behind her.

At first, Tony's shortcut didn't seem like much of a shortcut. He simply followed the road the bus took everyday. Fred pointed this out.

"Just wait," Tony told him. "You'll see."

And they did. As they passed a farmer's field, barren except for a few battered corn stalks left from the harvest last month, Tony turned. He led them up a rutted gravel road that led straight across the field and to the top of a hill. The others followed uncertainly.

"Are you sure we should be doing this?" Crystal asked. "I mean, this must be someone's private property."

"Don't worry about it," Tony said, grinning at her over his shoulder. "This is Mr. Koenig's field. He won't mind. He goes fishing with my dad all the time."

They followed the gravel road to the top of the hill. From there they could see several more rolling hills, and beyond that. . . .

"I can see the school's flagpole!" Stevie yelled, pointing.

"Sure," Tony said. "Told you. The school's just over that hill. We'll make it in plenty of time."

They trudged down the gravel road on the other side of the hill, where it ended at a rusty wire fence. Beyond it, thick, knee-high grass covered the ground, sweeping away to the tops of the surrounding hills like a green sea. Tony held down the wire fence so the others could step over.

As she crossed, Crystal asked, "Is this still your dad's friend's property?"

"I don't know," Tony confessed with a shrug. "Probably not, or it would be tilled. Maybe the school owns it."

Crystal was uneasy about being on private property without the owner's permission, but the school hadn't looked very far away from the top of the hill. If they *were* trespassing, it wouldn't be for very long, and if she refused to cross and went back now she would be late for school.

The thick grass on the other side of the fence was wet from the recent rains. Within half a minute, everyone's shoes were soaked.

"At least it washed away the mud," Lisa pointed out cheerfully.

Now that they were almost to the school and with time to spare, all their moods lightened. Fred and Stevie kicked their feet up high as they walked, trying to get each other wet, and Sheryl and Lisa sang songs from music class. Despite her wet feet, Crystal found herself enjoying the walk. The fresh air and exercise sure beat riding to school on the bus.

As she was surveying the surrounding country-side, Crystal noticed something odd. On their right, a hill rose to a crown of trees already stripped of their autumn leaves. The slope leading up to the trees was bare except for the thick grass, but halfway up was a spot where the ground didn't look right, as if a shadow were cast on it.

"What's that?" she asked, pointing.

Tony looked in the direction she was pointing. "Hey! It's a sinkhole," he said, starting to lope up the hillside. "Let's check it out."

Crystal frowned, but she checked her watch and found they had some time to spare. She had never seen a real sinkhole, although she had heard about them. She remembered a picture in a newspaper showing a car that had been swallowed up by a sinkhole in a parking lot. She and the others followed Tony up the hillside.

The sinkhole was a bowl-shaped depression about 20 feet across and about 10 feet deep at the bottom. The kids stood at the edge and looked, except for Tony, who ran right in.

"What is it?" Lisa asked.

"It's a sinkhole," Crystal explained. "Mr. Calvin told us about them in science class. You know how there are a lot of caves around here, from underground streams eating through the limestone? Well, sometimes the caves get so close to the surface that they collapse. Then the ground on top just sinks like this. It probably happened because of all the rain we've had recently."

"Hey! Check this out!" Tony called from the bottom of the sinkhole. He was on his hands and knees, and with a wriggle he disappeared into the ground. Crystal and the others stared in silent surprise. After a moment, Tony's head reappeared. "Come on down. There's a big cave in here."

Crystal checked her watch again. She felt uneasy, but they had time, and she had never been in a real cave. She made her slippery way down the side of the sinkhole to the bottom. There the hole in the earth was easily visible, though the tall grass had hidden it from above. It was a couple of feet across. Stevie and Fred crawled right through. Crystal was a little more reluctant. She didn't like small spaces. But when she put her head through the hole, she found that after a foot or so the cave opened wide. It was like crawling into a dark basement, with chill air seeping through her clothes and her hands and knees scrabbling on cold, damp stone.

The only light came from the hole, and at first Crystal couldn't see anything else. She could tell that the others were clustered around the hole, as she could barely make out their shoes. Stevie and Fred shouted to hear their voices echoing away into the distance until Tony told them to stop.

"My eyes are starting to get used to the dark," he said. Crystal could hear the scrape of his shoes on the stone floor as he walked deeper into the cave.

Stevie and Fred were at the hole, trying to convince Sheryl and Lisa to come in, but the two girls wouldn't hear of it. Crystal found that her eyes were adjusting to the darkness too, and she could see Tony's silhouette moving in the deeper blackness. She started to make out the long, pointy shapes of stalactites and stalagmites growing from the ceiling and floor, and she noticed something else too: a number of oblong shapes on the floor whose straight lines and edges seemed out of place among the curves and irregular surfaces in the cave. Tony was staggering among them.

"Are you okay, Tony?" she asked, concerned by the awkward way he moved.

"Yeah, why?" he replied, but his voice came from far to the left of the form she had seen moving among the oblong shapes.

She sucked in a panicked breath, but before she could utter a word Tony screamed.

"Get out! Get out! Get out!" he yelled.

Stevie and Fred both dived for the hole at the same time and wedged themselves in it. Crystal peered into the darkness in the direction of Tony's voice and heard a scuffling sound. She looked back to where she had seen the unidentified silhouette she had thought was Tony, and her blood turned to ice. She now saw several silhouettes, the closest only a few yards away.

"Hurry up!" she shrieked at Fred and Stevie as the two of them continued to try to wriggle through the hole at the same time.

"There's something else in here!" came Tony's panicked voice. "It tried to grab me, but—" His voice choked off with a grunt.

"Come on!" Crystal shouted. She grabbed Fred and pulled him back, freeing Stevie to squeeze through the hole. Then she pushed Fred toward it. She looked over her shoulder and saw the figures in the darkness getting closer. Dry, brittle scraping sounds carried through the thick shadows as they moved, almost on her. Terrified at the thought of their touching her, Crystal plunged through the hole, propelling Fred ahead of her.

She crawled across the grass outside, blinking at the sudden brightness, until she was well away from the hole. When she turned back toward it, she was relieved to see Tony crawling out, his eyes huge and his face white. But as his legs started to emerge, something jerked him to a stop. Then his legs were pulled back in.

"Help!" Tony yelled. But as the others moved to grab him, his body disappeared until only his hands remained in sight, gripping the sides of the hole with white knuckles. And then, with a sudden jerk, they too were gone. Tony's screams echoed from the hole, and then all was quiet.

The children stared in stunned horror.

Crystal looked at Fred and Stevie. "Tell me this is another one of Tony's stupid jokes." But she could tell from Stevie's tears and Fred's shaking hands that this was no joke, as much as she wanted it to be.

"Come on," she said, making her way up the side of the sinkhole and pulling herself up to the ground above. "We have to go get help."

The others obeyed her orders without question and followed her the rest of the way to school without saying a word.

Crystal led the principal, the vice principal, one of the gym teachers, and the janitor back to the hillside. She told them that Tony had gone into a cave at the bottom of a sinkhole but didn't mention the *things* that were inside. The other kids had stayed at the school, too upset to do much more than stare blankly into space.

From the time she left the sinkhole to the time she returned with the principal and the others, no more than half an hour had passed, but the hillside was now a perfectly smooth field of grass; the sinkhole was gone.

She led them to the exact place, stomping on the ground to try to find a weak or hollow spot, but it all seemed perfectly solid. The adults looked around doubtfully for some sign of the sinkhole or the missing boy.

"You're sure this is the spot?" the principal asked, looking red and out of breath in his suit and tie.

"It was right here," she insisted.

He frowned, looking around. "Okay, here's what we'll do. Each of you pick a direction and start walking. Watch out for holes hidden in the grass. After five minutes, we'll meet back here."

The principal chose to walk toward the top of the hill, taking Crystal with him. "We should get a better look from up there," he said. "Maybe you'll notice something familiar."

It took only a few minutes to reach the trees at the top. When the principal stopped to survey the hillside below, Crystal thought she saw something through the trees and took a few more steps to be sure. On the other side of the hill, directly opposite where the sinkhole had been, she saw a cemetery filled with dozens of gravestones. Crystal froze in horror. She suddenly realized that the oblong shapes she had seen in the cave were coffins, and that meant that the figures moving in the darkness must have been. . . .

"I don't see any sign of Tony," the principal said, facing away from her and not noticing her trembling hands. "Do you?"

"No," Crystal whispered.

And as she looked down at the cemetery she became certain that no living person would ever see Tony again.

DARYL'S DARK SIDE

⊷ ⊶⟐⟠ ⊷

DARYL PRESSED HIS FACE AGAINST THE PHOTOCOPIER glass and puffed out his cheeks like a blowfish. Then he groped around until his fingers found the PRINT button and pressed it. The machine hummed into action. A piercing light passed across his eyes. Daryl removed his face from the photocopier and snatched up the page that came out.

His best friend, Pete, snickered from his position by the hall door, where he was standing lookout. The other door led to the faculty lounge, but they had already checked and no one was in there.

"I can't believe we're doing this," Pete said.

Daryl gave him a bored look, as if he did things like sneak into the teachers' workroom all the time. And he did.

"It's second period," he told Pete. "What are we supposed to do? Sit in Ms. Gordon's class while she babbles on and on about Christopher Columbus? Not while I have a stash of forged hall passes—thanks to the wonderful machines here in the teachers' workroom."

He patted the back pocket of his jeans, which was bulging with the passes, freshly copied on the photocopier and cut on the paper cutter. Now that the business part of their mission was accomplished, he was amusing himself by photocopying his face with different expressions.

Pete took a swig of the soda Daryl had gotten for him from the vending machine in the faculty lounge. "You're unbelievable. No wonder they call you Daring Daryl!"

That had been his nickname since the second grade. He caused more trouble than any three other kids, and he had never spent one minute in detention. He could throw a spitball so casually that even a teacher looking right at him wouldn't notice, but he would react so dramatically that anyone retaliating against him was sure to be caught whether they hit him or not.

Daryl didn't just pass notes in class. When the teacher's attention was elsewhere, he would dash across the room and spring over desks to deliver his notes personally. When the teacher looked, he would duck behind other students or sit nonchalantly in a handy vacant desk until the teacher looked away again. One time when he was caught out in the open he made Mr. Fields believe he was retrieving a dropped pencil— three rows away from his own desk!

Daryl shrugged modestly. "It's a gift." Then he scowled at the page in his hand. "Too bad I'm not as good with photocopiers."

He turned the page around to show Pete that it was mostly white except for a dark ring where his lips had been pressed to the glass.

"It's set too light," Pete said. He put his soda on the machine, then pressed a button a few times. "Now try it."

Daryl lifted the cover and once again applied his face to the glass. He started to grope around with his free hand, searching for the PRINT button. As he hit it, his wrist brushed something and knocked it over. The machine hummed smoothly to life as before, but then it made a horrible grinding sound and started to shake like an unbalanced washing machine. Then came the light, brighter than before and lasting longer than the previous brief flash. Daryl felt as if it were going right through him. He jumped back from the machine, blinking and blinded. The nose-wrinkling smell of burning electronics filled the room.

"Oh man," Pete said, "we've done it now. Come on!"

"I can't see," Daryl hissed, but already his vision was starting to return.

Pete grabbed his arm. "This way," he said, panic giving his voice a high edge. "Quick, before someone comes!"

Daryl staggered after his friend. They made it out to the hall, and the door closed behind them. Daryl blinked hard a few more times, now able to see much better, though afterimages of the bright light still throbbed over the rest of the world.

"We can go to the auditorium and hide backstage until next class," Pete said. "If Ms. Gordon didn't notice we sneaked out, no one'll ever guess we were the ones who fried the photocopier."

"Yeah," Daryl agreed, but then he stopped and looked back at the door to the teachers' workroom.

"What are you doing?" Pete demanded in a frantic whisper.

"I have to go back," Daryl said, striding away from his friend and back to the scene of the crime.

"You're nuts! Why?" Pete had to trot alongside Daryl to keep up with him.

"I've got to get that page," Daryl explained calmly. "If they find the machine fried with a photocopy of my face still in it, even I am going to have a tough time getting out of it."

"You can't go back in there," Pete protested. "Look, they'll never be able to tell it's you."

Daryl shook his head. "I can't take that chance."

He put his hand on the doorknob. "Why don't you wait for me in the auditorium? If anyone's in here, I'll say I wrecked the photocopier by myself. No sense in both of us getting nailed."

Pete hesitated, obviously not wanting to abandon his friend. But neither did he want to risk punishment from both the school and his parents. He wished Daryl good luck and bolted down the hallway.

"Daring Daryl doesn't need luck," Daryl murmured. Then he opened the door a crack.

Smoke still hung in the quiet workroom, but he didn't see anyone. He started opening the door wider and was startled to hear the room's other door closing. He opened the door wider and found the room empty. He was puzzled by the closing of the other door—if someone had discovered the broken machine, they would have taken a few minutes to see what the problem was.

But the empty room worked in Daryl's favor, so he didn't question it too closely. He stepped to the machine and checked its output tray. It was empty. That troubled him. Had someone come in, found the photocopy, and then left right away to find him? That explanation didn't make a lot of sense. More likely, the dying machine hadn't been able to make the copy at all.

Well, Daryl decided, if it had, he would find out about it soon enough. He tossed Pete's soda can into the trash and casually walked out of the room to join his friend.

—⇒◦⇐—

Daryl rested easier as the day went on, sure that he had gotten away with yet another piece of mischief. But after lunch, when a voice over the intercom summoned him to the principal's office, he was sure school officials had figured out who was responsible for the photocopier's meltdown.

The principal, Mr. Borstein, was waiting for him in the main office. He had thick, dark hair and a perpetual scowl that made him a dead ringer for some dead Russian dictator pictured in Daryl's history textbook. Daryl had once made dozens of copies of the picture with funny speech balloons and spread them all over the school, but any urge he had to smile at the memory was quashed when Mr. Borstein glared at him with his full attention.

"We'll talk in my office," he said, leading the way.

Daryl plodded after him, his mind working frantically to come up with an excuse. Then one suddenly came to him: He had been walking past the workroom and smelled smoke. When he opened the door, he had seen the photocopier on fire! Thinking fast, he extinguished the flames with soda but then was afraid he would be blamed, and so he fled. He wasn't a troublemaker—he was a hero!

"Daryl," Mr. Borstein said, "I'm very disappointed we have to have this conversation. You've never had to come see me before, and by all accounts you're a well-behaved young man."

"Wait, Mr. Borstein, I can explain," Daryl interrupted confidently. "You see, I was walking by and I smelled smoke—"

"So you threw a full bowl of vanilla pudding at Jack Fraser," Mr. Borstein finished for him, clearly not believing a word Daryl had said. "You thought perhaps his hair was on fire and that the pudding would put it out. That's very creative thinking, Daryl."

"Wait," Daryl protested. "Pudding? I didn't throw pudding at anyone." It was the kind of thing he *would* do, but he hadn't even been in the cafeteria during lunch. He had sneaked outside to play hacky-sack with Pete.

"There's no use lying," Mr. Borstein went on. "Mr. Calderwell saw you do it."

"But I didn't," Daryl said, mystified.

There was no convincing Mr. Borstein, however, and after listening to a 10-minute lecture on lunchroom behavior he received his very first detention—for something he didn't even do. Still, he decided, it was a lot better than having Mr. Borstein find out that he had ruined an expensive piece of office equipment.

———❖———

Detention turned out to be just as boring as Daryl had heard. He served his hour after school—one of the five he had been sentenced for the mysterious pudding incident, and walked home still puzzled. But, more than puzzled, he was hungry. He walked in the back door of the house into the kitchen. The warm aroma of baking filled the air. His mom sat at the table, reading the newspaper.

"Something smells good," he said. "Can I have a little piece to hold me until dinner?"

The newspaper lowered to reveal his mom wearing a glare that made Mr. Borstein's seem friendly.

"You have a lot of nerve asking me that, young man," she said, her anger making her speak very quickly.

"What?" he said. "What did I—if it's about the detention—"

She rose, throwing the paper onto the table in a mess of loose pages. "You want to know what you did?" She grabbed his arm and dragged him to the trash can. Daryl looked to the bottom, where a wrecked blueberry pie with one slice out of it rested among the eggshells and coffee grounds. "Sneaking a piece of pie without asking is one thing, but to throw the rest away? That's the most thoughtless, inconsiderate, wasteful thing I've ever heard of."

"But . . . but . . . I didn't do it," Daryl finally stammered, almost too shocked for words.

His mom laughed harshly. "Then who did?"

Daryl recovered enough to realize he could get out of this—he had an alibi. "I don't know," he said, "but it couldn't have been me. I had to stay after school for the past hour. Ask Mr. Borstein."

"Nice try," his mom huffed, "but I saw you come home an hour ago. I don't know what's come over you, Daryl, but it has me very upset. Now go upstairs until your dad gets home and we have a chance to talk about this."

Daryl couldn't believe it. His mom had to be mistaken about seeing him come home, but he didn't see how he could help himself by arguing about it now. He just grabbed his book bag and went upstairs as she had told him. Twice in one day he had been accused of something he hadn't done. It wasn't fair.

He opened his bedroom door and went inside. As he turned to close it, he froze. There, standing behind the door and smiling like a lottery winner was . . . himself.

"Mom sounded pretty mad," his twin said, stepping out of the corner. "Can't really blame her, though. I mean, wasting a whole pie like that, that's pretty bad."

"But I didn't do it," Daryl said distantly, still stunned.

"Of course you didn't do it," his twin snapped back over his shoulder as he opened the window. "I did, you idiot."

"But why? Who are you?"

His twin shrugged, smiling evilly. "I did it because I felt like it. And who am I?" He threw one leg over the windowsill. "Why, I'm you, stupid. Don't wait up."

And then he vanished outside. Daryl went to the window but saw no sign of his twin. He collapsed to the floor, trying to get hold of himself and figure out what was happening to his life.

———◆———

After his parents grounded him for a week, Daryl decided that what was happening to his life was that it was going down the toilet. But at least now he knew who to blame. He had a double. And he had only one explanation for how that had come to happen. He shared it with Pete the next morning when they were ditching second period backstage in the auditorium.

"It had to be the photocopier," Daryl said. "When I went back to get the photocopy, someone else was leaving through the other door. It must have been him."

Old sets for plays, volleyball nets, and Ping-Pong tables cluttered the backstage area, which was sealed off from the rest of the auditorium by heavy curtains. No one used it this time of year, making it the perfect place to hide out. Pete was sitting on the edge of a Ping-Pong table, looking skeptical.

"You can't make a copy of an actual person," Pete said. "It's impossible."

"I know," Daryl said, "but the soda and the sparks and everything must have done something. I don't know how, but it happened. Look, Pete, you have to believe me. No one else does."

Daryl watched his friend earnestly. He couldn't blame Pete. He probably wouldn't believe such a story if he hadn't seen the double himself. But he so very desperately needed someone to believe him.

Pete started to speak but was interrupted by the intercom. A familiar voice announced, "Attention, this is your captain speaking. This school has struck an iceberg and is sinking. All crew and passengers should proceed immediately to the lifeboats. And watch out for sharks."

The look on Pete's face as he struggled to understand what Daryl was up to changed during the intercom message. With obvious shock, he said, "That's your voice."

Daryl nodded.

Mr. Borstein's angry rumble now came over the intercom: "Daryl Brigham, report back to the office immediately. Daryl Brigham—*now*."

Daryl cringed.

"Do you want me to go along and say you were with me?" Pete offered.

Daryl shook his head. "They wouldn't believe us, and we'd both get in trouble."

Pete looked relieved. "Okay, but why is your double doing all this stuff?"

"I don't know," Daryl admitted. "He's way more out of control than I ever was, and he doesn't even try not to get caught. I guess because he knows I'll get the blame."

Pete snapped his fingers with sudden inspiration. "He's your dark side," he said.

"He's what?"

"He's your dark side. Remember how I adjusted the photocopier to make the copies darker? It must have brought out your dark side."

"That's stupid," Daryl said weakly.

Daryl received a lecture on responsibility and another three days of detention from Mr. Borstein for the intercom announcement. During the remainder of the day, Becky Camden yelled at him for dumping cottage cheese in her lunch box, Ms. Franklin told him that if he ever again made faces at her as he walked past her room he would be sorry, and Darren Tate dumped Daryl's books and kicked them down the hallway to "get even for this morning."

His double had been busy. As Daryl sat in detention after school, watching the second hand crawl around the face of the clock on the wall, he wondered what his double was up to *now.* What new disaster would he have to face when he got home?

As Daryl wallowed in his dark thoughts, the kid at the desk next to him whispered, "Hey! Daring Daryl!"

He checked up front, but Mr. Kellogg was buried behind the newspaper. Whispering was safe as long as they didn't get carried away.

"What?" He recognized the kid from the hallways but didn't know his name. He must have been in a lower grade.

"What are you doing here?" the kid asked. "I mean, you're *Daring Daryl*. You're a legend. You're my hero. How did they catch you?"

Daryl felt flattered and a little embarrassed. "I sort of outsmarted myself," he answered.

The rustle of newspaper from the front of the classroom ended the conversation, but it had started Daryl thinking. He *was* Daring Daryl. Okay, he was going through a rough time, but he was smart and clever. If anyone could think of a way out of this, he could. He spent the rest of detention thinking about it, and by the time Mr. Kellogg released him and the others he had a plan.

The way he saw it, the trouble was not that he had a double, but that nobody else knew about it—except for Pete, and he didn't count. In fact, if everyone knew he had a mischievous double, he could get away with all kinds of stuff by saying his dark side had done it.

So the first thing he had to do was convince his parents. With them on his side, he'd have a much easier time of convincing everyone at school. And how to do that? He could think of only one way.

Daryl wasted time until after five o'clock, when he was sure his father would be home. He wanted to prove his double's existence to both parents at once; after the first time, his double would be a lot warier.

He sneaked into the house and upstairs, where he could hear his parents talking in their bedroom. Then he went to his own bedroom and slipped inside. As he had hoped, his double was there, just as he had been yesterday after school.

"You're home late," the double observed cheerfully from where it played a handheld video game on his bed. "What's the matter? Get in a little trouble?"

Daryl chuckled. "Yeah, something like that."

"That's rough," the double said, standing and chucking the game into the trash. "I'd hate to be you." It laughed evilly as it headed toward the window, just as it had yesterday.

"Not so fast!" Daryl said, and he leaped on his double. He got it in a headlock from behind and dragged it to the floor. If they were the same in all ways, they would have the same strength. Neither would be able to beat the other, but Daryl should be able to hold his double in place long enough for his plan to work.

"Mom! Dad!" he shouted. "In here, in the bedroom!"

The sound of their footsteps responded, and Daryl smiled in triumph as he braced himself against his double's struggles. But the double stopped struggling and gave a small laugh.

"Sucker," it said, and then it turned into a fine black powder, which covered Daryl and the carpet around him.

The bedroom door flew open, revealing Daryl's parents, their eyes wide in alarm.

"Daryl," his father said, "what's wrong, and what is that mess?"

Daryl shook the black powder from his arms. It was the black toner they used in photocopiers, he realized.

"I—uh . . ." Daryl started to think of an excuse and drew a blank.

"This is it, Daryl," his father said. "I don't know what your problem is, but it's going to stop. Do you understand me? Now get this mess cleaned up and then come downstairs. We're going to have a long talk about this, and you're going to be in trouble for a long, long time."

With that his father closed the door. The black powder started to shift and move on its own and then swirled around in the air, once again forming a perfect duplicate of Daryl.

"Nice try," his double said with a superior grin. "But I knew you were going to do it. It's what *I* would have done. So now you know that you'll never be able to convince anyone else I'm around. Get used to it, Daryl. Get used to being blamed and punished and yelled at, because I'm only getting started. Fortunately for you, I like having you around to take the blame. But if you do anything else to make me mad . . . well, let's just say there's something else besides the black-powder trick that we don't have in common: I don't sleep. You have to. And if you annoy me again, the next time you go to sleep you're not going to wake up, and no one's ever going to miss you. Got it? Now I've got trouble to cause."

With a final wave, the double went to the window and vanished once again. Daryl dropped his head into his hands in despair. He didn't even look up when he heard someone coming up the stairs and his bedroom door opening.

"Okay, Daryl," his mother said, anger firing her voice. "Do you want to tell me why you spray-painted the neighbor's cat blue?"

All Daryl could do was say "I don't know" and wait for his punishment.

GAME OVER

BOBBY HATED FLEA MARKETS. MORE THAN GOING to the dentist or school or toxic-breathed Aunt Nancy's, he *hated* going to flea markets.

But every Sunday morning that's exactly where his parents dragged him and his twin sister, Kaitlyn. On days when the weather was nice, they would go to the big outside flea market at the drive-in movie theater. On cold and rainy days, they journeyed to Ready Rosco's Market in Grange County.

At the drive-in it was always hot, with dust choking the air. He could feel it coating the inside of his mouth and his throat. When he tried to spit it out, his mother yelled at him, saying that it was rude to spit.

His parents marched him up and down endless rows of junk—old farmers selling tomatoes and corn from the backs of trucks, grannies with dozens of knitted toaster covers and toilet-paper cozies, men stained dark with grease selling rusty nails and screws in old coffee cans, and all sorts of other people with every kind of junk imaginable displayed on rickety card tables or on worn blankets spread on the ground.

Bobby couldn't believe people paid money for any of this stuff. Ancient TVs and vacuum cleaners that probably didn't work, scratched vinyl records crammed in cardboard boxes, ugly furniture missing legs and losing stuffing—to him it all looked as if it had been stolen from somebody's curb on trash day.

But after spending a few hours trudging through the junk at the drive-in, Bobby could always count on a stop at the snow-cone stand. His parents acted as if it was some kind of treat, but come on—this was survival. After marching through the endless dusty rows, dying of thirst was a real concern.

While they ate their snow cones, his parents would excitedly show everyone what they had bought. His mother always picked up old saw blades, both the long ones with wooden handles and the round ones that sometimes were as big as a pizza. She took the rusty things home and painted cheerful little scenes on them. A few hung in their living room, but the rest she gave away or donated to craft sales. Bobby didn't see the point at all.

His father collected old 45-rpm records, which he played on a jukebox in their basement. He usually ended up with a bagful, which he'd proudly flip through while they ate their snow cones. He would read the names of music groups Bobby had never heard of and sing bits of songs that made Bobby cringe.

Even Kaitlyn had something to show for her time at the flea market—clothes for her dolls or a tiny china teapot that had caught her eye. Their parents would look at what she had bought and *ooh* and *ah* while Bobby rolled his eyes.

Bobby never bought anything, and they knew better than to ask. He had money. That was no problem. He got the same allowance as Kaitlyn, $10 a week, even though he had to do all the tough chores like mowing the lawn while she got off with easy stuff like washing the dishes. But there was only one thing Bobby wanted: new video games. They were expensive, but every month or so he saved up enough money to buy a new one. And no flea-market junk would ever convince him to spend any of his precious video-game money.

——◆——

It was on a rainy October morning that Bobby changed his mind. It seemed as if he had just gotten out of school on Friday afternoon and here it was Sunday morning already. Only 24 hours of freedom before he had to go back to school.

After breakfast, he slipped down to the basement, where his Phantacom 3000 game system was all ready to go. The glow of the 35-inch TV screen as an aircraft carrier loomed across it provided the only light in the dark basement. Bobby held the game pad, ready to take off from the flight deck and blast some UFOs. He'd had the game, *Alien Dogfighters,* for a week now and was already bored with it, but his friend Tim had gotten the high score, and Bobby wouldn't rest until he had beaten it. It was his game, he reasoned; the high score should be his. He got the green light and hit the button to launch his jet fighter.

"Everybody ready to go to the flea market?" his dad called from upstairs.

Bobby grimaced. This was so unfair. He was 12 years old. He should be able to stay home and do whatever he wanted. But he knew that it wouldn't do any good to argue.

"This is family time, time to spend together," he would be told, and that would be the end of it.

He threw down the game pad and turned off the Phantacom 3000. It looked as if he wasn't going to have any fun at all today.

⟫◦⟪

"I guess it's time to head for Rosco's," Bobby's father pronounced from behind the wheel of the car.

"Great," Bobby replied, scowling out the window. The icy rain ruled out going to the drive-in, which meant their first trip to Ready Rosco's Market since last spring. As bad as the drive-in was, at least they could get snow cones there. At Ready Rosco's, they sold only cheap hot dogs, bags of potato chips, and cans of soda. Rosco's was twice as far away as the drive-in, all the way out in Grange County, which meant another hour of freedom lost from Bobby's weekend. Bobby settled into a sulk, looking out the car window.

"I hope that nice old lady is there," Kaitlyn said. "The one who makes her own Barbie clothes. I got some great outfits the last time we were there."

"You never know," her mom said. "It's been so long since we've been there, a lot might have changed. New people with new things to sell."

"That's right," her father agreed. "That's the good thing about having been away so long. There might be all kinds of people with Barbie clothes—or saw blades for your mother, or records for me . . . or even something for Bobby."

Bobby snorted. "Yeah, right. Maybe if the place burned down and they built a mall there."

But the others wouldn't let themselves be bothered by his attitude. "You never know," his mother repeated.

———◆———

Rosco's was as bad as Bobby remembered. They parked in the grassy field and then trudged through the rain toward the long, rambling building. It actually looked like a bunch of different buildings that had been set next to each other like dominos. Inside, it was like a maze.

The building they entered first was a long, low-roofed barn. Bobby guessed it used to be a chicken house. It sure smelled like it. The barn stretched on for a while and then joined with a long sheet-metal building with an oil-stained concrete floor. This building led into a huge warehouselike building that had a bunch of different exits. There was a cafeteria area here, with plywood tables and folding chairs, and this was where Bobby's family always split up and then met again later, so everyone wouldn't have to wait around while Bobby's father dug through boxes of records or while his mother talked to friends selling crafts.

"Okay," his dad said, holding up his wrist, "time to synchronize watches."

He made the same goofy spy-movie joke every time, as if their watches being a minute off would cause millions of people to die. Bobby didn't even look at his.

"We'll meet right back here in two hours," his father pronounced. "Ready? Break!"

The others headed off on their own individual treasure hunts. Bobby stood there for a moment, disgusted.

Even Kaitlyn happily hurried off, her ponytail bobbing behind her. Until a couple of years ago, she and Bobby used to hang out and kill time together, playing hide-and-seek in the crowd or tic-tac-toe on the plywood tables. But then she had started acting like one of *them*, like their parents, poking through the piles of junk looking for things to waste perfectly good money on.

Two hours to kill. Bobby decided he might as well walk around to make the time go faster. He wandered past a booth filled with nothing but wooden handles for hammers, axes, and shovels, then past another packed with musty paperback books shelved every which way in stacked milk crates.

He checked his watch: One minute gone.

Then, past a booth where a snoozing bald guy was selling old license plates, Bobby noticed an exit from the big center building that he didn't remember. There were a lot of exits, and things had changed quite a bit from last spring, but he was pretty sure that this gloomy corridor leading away and slightly downward had not been here before. Though he despised Rosco's Market, he knew the layout pretty well from playing hide-and-seek with Kaitlyn. This was new.

Not that this discovery excited him much, but he swerved toward the corridor anyway. At least finding out where it went would help him waste a little more time.

At first he was less than thrilled. The narrow corridor had cinder-block walls and a concrete ceiling that seemed to be holding up a great weight. That and the slight downward angle of the floor made it seem as if he were descending far beneath the surface of the earth. But that was silly.

The vendors here were new too. He passed by long tables filled with plants of types he couldn't identify, with long moist leaves that licked at his skin and seemed to try to grab him as he went by. They grew up to the low ceiling and smothered the lights so that the farther he walked, the darker it seemed to get. Past the plants, it was darker still. As he walked down an aisle of bubbling aquariums, he could barely see his way. In the black water, shadows moved, and he caught a glimpse of something with many teeth flickering past.

Then came an area so dark he had to feel his way along. His fingertips moved along the tops of tables, feeling first something scaly like snakeskin, then something smooth like leather—clothing, he assumed.

Bobby was feeling very nervous by now. His heart beat faster, and sweat was making his scalp prickle. He wouldn't have gone any farther except that he saw lights up ahead and didn't want to go back past the dark tables and the aquariums and the strange plants. He moved faster and faster toward the colored lights, which appeared small like jewels at first but quickly grew larger. He barely looked at the tables and displays as he passed them—gleaming metal tools and instruments like those doctors on TV used, powders and liquids in small glass bottles labeled with what looked like scribbles, blank pieces of stone of all sizes such as might be carved and polished to mark graves.

At first he paid little attention because he merely wanted to reach the lights and, hopefully, the rest of the flea market. Then he saw what the lights spelled, and he felt a surge of excitement. The neon sign over the booth read in colorful letters "VIDEO GAMES."

Bobby reached the well-lit booth. The walls here were made of huge stones and seemed ancient. The air was damp, like that in a cave. Bobby ignored this and eagerly studied the booth's orderly bins. There were sections for each kind of video game system, filled with all sorts of cartridges and controllers. There were bins for all of the Nintendo machines, ancient Ataris up through Jaguar, Sega Genesis and Saturn, Sony PlayStation . . . and there, the best of the best, the most powerful game machine of them all, the Phantacom 3000. Bobby rushed to the Phantacom bin and started flipping through the cartridges. They were in good shape—like new—and so inexpensive! He had paid two or three times as much for most of them.

Or for all of them—as it began to look as if they were all games he already owned. Then, at the very back, he came upon one he had never even *heard* of: *Destiny's Dungeon*. Unlike the others, the cartridge was worn and missing half its label. Other than the name and "4 Players Required," the remains of the label gave no information.

Bobby pulled it out and held it in his hands. He and his friends read all the video game magazines as soon as they hit the newsstands. They knew all the games that were out, which new ones were coming out, and when they would be available. But he had never heard about this one— maybe it was only sold in other countries—but if he hadn't heard of it, then his friends wouldn't have either. If he bought it, he would be the only one to own it. He liked the thought of that. But he turned it every which way and found no price. Nor were any prices posted above the bins. He turned to look around and found a sun-burned old man standing right behind him.

Bobby stepped back and almost screamed. The old man had no hair, and even his wrinkled scalp was so enflamed that it was almost glowing. He probably got sunburned at an outdoor flea market like the one at the drive-in, Bobby figured.

"Good morning, young man," the sun-burned man said. "If indeed morning it still be. It's so hard to tell down here. You're a Phantacom fan, I see."

"Yeah," Bobby said, the word coming out almost as a croak as he found his voice. "How much is this game?"

"Hm," the man murmured, squinting one eye as he gazed at Bobby appraisingly. "That would be $10, just as it says on the price tag."

"There isn't—" Bobby started to protest, but he stopped when he looked down and saw the hand-printed tag stuck to the cartridge in his hand. He must have missed it somehow, he figured, and then his excitement overwhelmed all other thoughts. He had spent all his money on *Alien Dogfighters* last week, but on Friday had received his allowance: He had exactly $10.

His parents often bragged about how they haggled and bargained to get better prices on items at the flea market, saying that this was half the fun of coming, but Bobby didn't care. He pulled the $10 bill from his wallet, handed it to the man, and started to leave with his purchase.

"Remember," the man called after him, "you need four players for that one."

Bobby turned to thank him but saw no sign of the sun-burned man among the bins of video games. He shrugged and headed away from the booth, too excited to think about anything else.

Just around a curve from the video game booth, a short flight of stairs led up into another of the flea market's many buildings, one that Bobby recognized. He checked his watch and was shocked to realize that his two hours were almost up. He hurried toward the cafeteria to meet his family and tell them what a treasure he had found.

———⊰◈⊱———

Bobby's mom and dad were so pleasantly surprised that he had bought something at the flea market—and that he was *smiling*—that they agreed to let him have his friends over as soon as they got home. He called Brad and Tim and Scott, who said they would be right over when he told them about the new game, and then he went down into the basement to wait.

He made good use of his time by hooking up all four controllers to the Phantacom 3000. Very few games allowed more than two people to play at the same time, which made *Destiny's Dungeon* even more of a find.

Tim arrived first, since he lived only a few houses away, and Scott arrived soon after, a bit damp from riding his bike in the rain but excited to play the new game. They turned on the Phantacom while they waited for Brad to see what the game was like, but all that showed on the screen was the message "Four players are required to play *Destiny's Dungeon.*"

They tried pressing the buttons on the fourth game pad, but the message remained on the screen.

"It must be able to tell that there're only three of us," Scott said.

Then Bobby's mom called down that he had a phone call. Bobby ran upstairs to take it.

"Hi, it's Brad," said the sulky voice on the other end of the line. "My mom says I can't come over until I finish my homework, and I haven't even started yet. So I guess I'm not coming."

Bobby hung up in disappointment. They had already learned that you couldn't play the game with only three people, and he was dying to play. It just wasn't fair. After all the flea markets he had suffered through, he deserved to have some fun.

Then he noticed Kaitlyn watching TV in the family room. He ran to his twin sister's side and said, "Hey, want to play my new video game with us?"

"No," she said, without taking her eyes off the screen.

"Oh, come on, you'll have fun."

"No, I won't," she said. "I hate playing video games with you. You always shoot me or run over me or whatever and I hardly get to play."

Bobby promised over and over that that wouldn't happen this time, crossed his heart and hoped to die, and finally she agreed to play. He led her excitedly back down to the basement. Tim and Scott looked a little skeptical about her playing, but after Bobby explained that Brad couldn't come they got the picture: If they wanted to play *Destiny's Dungeon*, they needed Kaitlyn.

The four of them hit their start buttons, and the game began with creepy music and a brief introduction about a princess being kidnapped and held in a dark dungeon by horrible creatures. Then the players got to pick their characters—Bobby chose a burly dwarf with an enormous ax—and the action started.

A wave of hideous ogres and trolls rushed at them from all sides in the dark dungeon chamber. The four kids screamed and cheered as their on-screen characters leaped into battle, Tim's wizard shooting fireballs, Scott's warrior swinging his sword, and Kaitlyn's centaur firing arrows. In half a minute, they had wiped out the last of their opponents. Each of the four characters had a status box with a life meter at the bottom of the screen. All of them were down some from wounds received during the battle, but Kaitlyn's was almost gone. Bobby knew she was going to die when the next battle started, but despite his promise he didn't really care. Now that they were playing it didn't matter if she got upset and left.

"This is really cool," Tim said, flexing his fingers in readiness for the next wave.

"Yeah," Scott agreed.

Bobby only grinned. Who would have thought he'd ever find something good at a flea market?

Ominous music announced the beginning of the next battle—more trolls and ogres, this time led by a ferocious Minotaur with a huge club. Bobby and the others waded into their midst.

As he had predicted, within seconds Kaitlyn's life meter ran out, and the words "GAME OVER" flashed over her status box. Bobby glanced over to see how she was taking it and saw her game pad resting on the floor.

"Where'd Kaitlyn go?" he asked.

"Look at that!" Tim said, pointing at the screen.

Bobby looked and saw that Kaitlyn's centaur had turned into . . . Kaitlyn. It was her voice, crying for help, that came from the television speakers. Several ogres grabbed her, and despite her struggles, carried her easily down a hallway and off the screen.

"What the—?" Scott replied.

"Fight! Fight!" Tim shouted as their life meters fell.

As Bobby's mind reeled—*his sister had somehow disappeared into the game*—his fingers flew automatically across the game pad. His alter ego on the screen spun the ax in wide circles, taking out many attackers. Tim and Scott fought grimly on as well, until the screen had been cleared and they had a moment to relax. Tim and Bobby still had half of their life left, but Scott's meter was almost gone.

"Tell me that didn't really happen," Tim said.

"It *couldn't* have happened," Scott replied.

Bobby shook his head slowly. "But it did."

"Maybe we should turn it off," Scott said.

"No," Bobby insisted. "We have to keep playing. Maybe if we beat the game we'll get Kaitlyn back." *And what*, he wondered, *am I going to do if we don't?*

Before the others could respond, the next wave of attackers appeared. There were twice as many ogres and trolls now, and two Minotaurs. The three boys were quiet except for the click of their fingers on the game pads.

Almost immediately, Scott's warrior was struck down. Bobby heard his game pad hit the basement floor but still didn't look away from the screen. There was Scott. A half dozen ogres and trolls grabbed his thrashing form and rushed him off the screen. Over his status box, the words "GAME OVER" flashed, just as they still did over Kaitlyn's.

Tim threw down his game controller and stood up. "I'm sorry, Bobby. I have to get out of here."

"No, wait," Bobby called after him. "We've got to keep playing. It's the only way."

But Tim was beyond reasoning. He started running up the stairs, shouting how sorry he was as he went. On the screen, his wizard stood idle, easy prey for monsters. His life meter plummeted.

The footsteps on the stairs and Tim's voice stopped abruptly. Bobby didn't have to look over his shoulder to know that Tim was gone. The ogres and trolls carried him away. Three of the four status boxes were now eclipsed by the flashing words "GAME OVER."

Bobby fought on, his fingers moving so quickly and desperately that his hands began to cramp. He slew both Minotaurs and dozens of trolls and ogres, but his life meter was dangerously low. As he killed the last ogre, a troll slashed him from behind, draining the last of his life.

Everything went dark and dizzy for a moment, and Bobby felt himself falling. Then he came to his senses sprawled on the cold stone floor. At first he thought he was back in that strange hall in the flea market—it smelled the same and had the same cool, damp feel to the air, the same ancient stones in the walls. But then he saw the enormous ax gripped in his hands. The troll, 8 feet tall with tusks like dirty knives, kept a wary distance as Bobby tried to lift the ax. He wondered what it was waiting for as tears of frustration squeezed from his eyes, and then he saw them— the dozens of other trolls and ogres. In the far shadows he glimpsed their master, his bald, red head glowing like lava, and Bobby could feel the words flashing in his mind: "GAME OVER."

SHOPLIFTERS WILL BE KILLED AND EATEN

ALL DAY JEREMY LOOKED FORWARD TO ONE THING: making his weekly trip to Memories of Tomorrow after school. Today was Tuesday, and every Tuesday Memories, the town's best comic book and trading card store, received its shipment of new comics and other merchandise.

Jeremy's friends and classmates would be lined up for the new comics, but comics didn't interest Jeremy. He loved dinosaurs. He watched movies about them, read books about them, and built models of them. The walls of his room were covered with dinosaur posters. His shelves were packed with dinosaur action figures. He even had dinosaur sheets on his bed. His greatest dream was that someday he would be a paleontologist, studying dinosaurs—or at least what was left of them—firsthand.

Half the items in his room had come from Memories of Tomorrow, but it had been a while since the store had gotten anything new for him to buy. In his opinion, Stephen, the owner and manager, gave too much of his attention to comics and science fiction books and not enough to dinosaurs.

Stephen was famous for being able to get almost anything his customers wanted, no matter how old or how hard to find. He had gotten a rare early *Superman* comic for Jimmy Feldman's dad, and in excellent condition. Stephen himself had a signed first edition of H. G. Wells's classic science fiction novel *The Time Machine* on display in the store, though it wasn't for sale. If he could get things like that, how hard could it be to get a few new dinosaur-related items every week? Jeremy was a good customer and deserved good treatment.

After school, he rode his bike to the town square, where numerous colorful shops surrounded the historic courthouse. Then he turned onto a side street and chained his bicycle to a parking meter in front of Santino's Italian Restaurant. Next to the restaurant entrance, a set of concrete steps led down. A hand-painted sign with an arrow pointing downward read "Memories of Tomorrow."

Jeremy descended the steps, feeling a familiar surge of anticipation. This could be the week! He pushed his way into the store and lingered around the front by the T-shirt rack while his eyes adjusted to the dimness. Since it was below street level, the store had no windows, and it was lit by only a few fluorescent lights. Countless posters covered the walls, where they were visible, and shelves displaying comics, paperbacks, models, and all sorts of other merchandise packed most of the available floor space. A row of glass cases formed a counter on one side, behind which Stephen worked. He and his assistant, Carl, were dealing with the line of people there to buy newly acquired comics, but he waved when he saw Jeremy.

"Hey, buddy," he called. "I have a little something you might be interested in."

Jeremy made his way to the counter as Stephen rooted around behind it. Stephen was a tall, thin man with a long, dark ponytail and a goatee. He usually wore T-shirts with comic book characters on them, like the Spawn shirt he was wearing today.

"We finally got the *Dino-Fever* cards," Stephen said as he searched. "Those are already out on the floor. But there was—aha!"

He stood from behind the counter and unrolled a poster for Jeremy's inspection.

"Wow, T. Rex!" Jeremy cheered. But as he studied the king of the dinosaurs, something struck him as wrong. "It's blue," he said.

Stephen looked at the poster and shrugged. "Yeah, but look at the quality of the artwork. Reynolds Sinclair painted this image. It's a hundred times better than those other posters you've bought."

"Yeah," Jeremy said, "but it's blue."

"Sure it's blue," Stephen said. "Look, you're up on your dinosaur reading. You know that scientists don't really know what color dinosaurs were. All they've got are bones."

"Yeah, but T. Rex was *not* blue," Jeremy protested. "It just doesn't look right."

"You've seen *Jurassic Park* too many times, buddy," Stephen told him, getting a laugh from the dozen people standing in line for comics.

"I have not," Jeremy said, feeling his face turn red.

Stephen let the poster roll closed and held up one hand in a gesture of peace. "Okay, okay. If you don't want the poster, that's fine. But I know you plan on being a paleontologist. I've had some scientific training myself, and

I'll tell you, if you're going to be a scientist, you've got to keep an open mind. And I'll tell you something else—Tyrannosaurus Rex *really was* blue."

"Yeah, right, Stephen," Jeremy said, turning away. "Like you know everything."

"No, not everything," Stephen said with a theatrical flourish of his hands, "but I do know an excellent poster when I see one, my close-minded little friend."

The people in line laughed louder this time. Jeremy snorted and walked away. His skin burned with anger and embarrassment.

Stephen doesn't know what he's talking about, Jeremy told himself. *He just likes to show off. See if I ever buy anything else here again.*

But as he headed for the door, he passed a rack containing boxes of all sorts of trading cards, including the new *Dino-Fever* cards. He bit his lip as he picked up one of the foil-wrapped packets. He had read about the cards and seen ads in magazines, but he hadn't been able to find them anywhere. The sample cards pictured in the ads looked really cool, and Jeremy yearned to see what the rest of the cards looked like. But he didn't want to give Stephen the satisfaction of getting his money or another chance to make fun of him.

Jeremy glanced at the counter, but Stephen wasn't paying any attention to him. He was too busy filling comic book orders and laughing with other customers—probably about Jeremy.

Jeremy slipped the cards into his jacket pocket.

Nothing happened. No bells or alarms, no shouts of "Stop, thief!" The light was so dim in the store that Stephen probably couldn't even make out his face, much less what he was doing.

Jeremy grabbed a handful of packets and stuck them in his pocket. Then he put another handful in his other pocket. He smiled at Stephen, who still didn't notice him, and at the stupid sign Stephen had hanging behind the counter that said "Shoplifters will be killed and eaten."

Then he turned and left the store. He walked back up the stairs to his bicycle. As he pedaled home, he thought not only about his many new *Dino-Fever* cards, but also about how he had gotten even with that smug jerk Stephen.

———◆———

For the next couple of days, Jeremy was nervous about having stolen the cards. Whenever he heard a car door slam outside his house, he thought it was the police coming to take him away. By the next Tuesday, he was getting over his guilt but still didn't go back to Memories of Tomorrow. He told himself it was because he thought Stephen was a jerk, but there was also a guilty fear in him that, as soon as he walked in, Stephen would accuse him of stealing the cards.

But by the Tuesday after that, Jeremy thought he was safe. There was no way that Stephen had seen what he had done, and he had so much stuff in his store he probably had no idea anything was even missing. Besides, Jeremy had spent two whole weeks with no new dinosaur stuff, and he was itching to go see if he could find something interesting at Memories. And though he had stolen quite a few cards, he still needed a few to complete his set. This time he would actually pay for them—unless Stephen was a jerk again.

Jeremy left his bike chained to the parking meter and went into the store. It didn't seem to have changed at all in two weeks. The usual Tuesday afternoon crowd was there waiting for their new comics, and Stephen and Carl were busy behind the counter. Jeremy started to look around, hoping that Stephen wouldn't notice him.

"Hey, buddy," Stephen called. "Good to see you. We missed you last week."

Jeremy wandered toward the counter. "Yeah, I wasn't feeling too good."

"It figures—the one week we get something I know you're going to be interested in."

Jeremy felt the stirrings of disappointment. He knew he should have come in last week. Stephen didn't suspect a thing about his shoplifting the cards. Now, because of his guilty conscience, he had missed something good.

"What was it?" Jeremy asked, now not sure if he even wanted to know.

Stephen gave him a sparkling smile. "Cheer up! I saved it for you. Come on, it's in back."

Stephen told Carl he'd be back in a minute and then came around the counter to lead Jeremy through the store to the stout door in the rear. Stephen flipped through a ring of keys. Jeremy glanced back at the others in the store, suddenly nervous. He had heard Carl talking one day when Stephen wasn't in the store. Someone asked about this door, and Carl said that nobody was allowed through it; even he didn't know what was behind it. So why would Stephen show Jeremy what was on the other side? Did it have something to do with his shoplifting? Was Stephen going to hold him back there until he confessed? Jeremy wanted to bolt out of the store, but that would really look suspicious. Before he could decide what to do, Stephen had the door open and was ushering him through.

On the other side was a workroom. Tools of all sorts, from heavy hammers to complex electronic measuring devices, lined the walls and cluttered workbenches. Boxes filled with odd bits of hardware and electronics were tucked wherever there was room. But Jeremy didn't have much time to look around. Stephen led him across the room to another door and into the room beyond. This second room was small, no more than 10 feet square, with bare walls painted silver. The only furniture in the room was a small desk by the door with a computer on it. Stephen sat down at the computer and started to type.

"Jeremy," he said as he typed, "I believe I owe you an apology for the last time you were here. I can be a little thick-headed sometimes, but after you didn't come last week I realized that you were probably angry with me and that you had every right to be."

An apology was the last thing Jeremy had expected, and in his relief he rushed to accept it. "That's okay, really."

"No," Stephen said, "no, it's not. But I'm going to make it up to you." He turned and smiled at Jeremy. "Right now." He tapped one final key, and it felt as if the whole building had jumped. Jeremy staggered, looking around wildly as if the roof might cave in, but everything was still.

"What was that?" Jeremy asked.

"That," Stephen answered as he stood, "is a secret. One I'm going to share with you. Come on."

He opened the door and led Jeremy back out into the workroom—only it wasn't a workroom anymore. The bare basement room was empty except for a table and a couple of wooden boxes. Stephen picked up two long overcoats from the table and tossed one to Jeremy.

"Put that on," he said. "It's going to be a good deal colder outside than you remember. It will help hide your clothes too."

Jeremy was confused but did as he was told, slipping into the heavy woolen coat and buttoning the old-fashioned buttons. "Why do I need to hide my clothes?" he asked.

"So they don't draw unwanted attention," Stephen answered. "Come along."

He led Jeremy through the other door back into the store—only the store was also gone. The basement here was empty except for a large pile of coal and a monstrous iron furnace that glowed with heat.

"My secret is this," Stephen said as he led Jeremy across the room. "You know how I'm able to find so many rare old treasures for so many of my customers?"

They reached the exit and started up the steps to street level.

"Yes," Jeremy said.

"I do it by going back in time, to when those items were new and easy to come by. That room behind the store is a time machine."

They reached the top of the steps. Jeremy's bike was gone, the parking meters were gone, the Italian restaurant was gone. It was snowing, though it had been 70 degrees when Jeremy had arrived at the store. The cars that lined the street looked enormous and overinflated, like cars out of an old movie.

"Welcome," Stephen said, "to the 1940s."

Stephen led the way up the street toward the courthouse. Jeremy marveled at how the square was so different and yet still so familiar. The old movie theater that had burned down years ago was all lit up and was advertising a new John Wayne film. The traffic lights at the main intersection were gone, replaced by a policeman directing traffic in an old-fashioned uniform. On one corner was a wooden newsstand Jeremy had never seen before, and that was Stephen's destination.

"Good day, Mr. Fink," Stephen said to the man behind the counter.

"And to you too, sir," answered the man, digging beneath the counter. "I've got your order right here. Though what a grown man like yourself sees in these funny books is beyond me."

He handed over a small bundle bound with string. On top Jeremy saw a new copy of a Batman comic book.

"They're not for me," Stephen said, handing the man some money. "They're for a . . . friend."

"Sure, they are," the man answered. "You keep yourself warm tonight, sir. It's supposed to be a cold one. A good night to stay in and listen to the radio by the fire."

Stephen thanked the man and then led Jeremy back toward the store—or to where the store would be in 50 years.

"This is amazing," Jeremy said as they walked. "How long have you been doing this?"

"A few years," Stephen answered as they walked. "I was studying physics in college and came up with my theory of time travel. After I got it working, I realized I could do whatever I wanted, and what I really wanted was to open up a comic book shop. Since then, I've traveled in time to find items for my customers and just for my own enlightenment. It's fascinating, the things you can learn."

They reached their building and returned to the basement. Following Stephen's example, Jeremy took off his heavy overcoat and left it on the table. Then both went back into the time-travel room. Stephen sat down at the computer and began to type. When he finished, the room again seemed to jump. He directed Jeremy to the door. Jeremy opened it and stepped outside.

He had expected to find himself back in the workroom, but instead he found himself outside in a steamy jungle. He sank to his ankles in the marshy ground and found himself surrounded by the fronds of gigantic ferns. The buzz of insects filled the air. He glanced back, where the doorway into the time-travel room appeared to float in midair. Stephen stood in the doorway, holding a small gun pointed at Jeremy!

"Don't worry," Stephen said, waving the gun. "I'm a man of my word, and I promise not to hurt you. I just want to make sure I have your complete attention. You probably haven't had enough time to consider all the ramifications of time travel, so allow me to point out another use. When I discovered that someone had stolen a whole pile of *Dino-Fever* cards from my store, I went back in time and hid a video camera to catch the thief in the act."

The ground shook, but not from travel through time. Jeremy looked around but could see nothing through the thick vegetation.

"Perhaps you've noticed the sign in my shop," Stephen continued conversationally. "The one that says 'Shoplifters will be killed and eaten'?" He glanced around as the trembling of the ground grew stronger, and he smiled. "As I said, I'm a man of my word."

He stepped back and started to shut the door. Jeremy screamed for him to stop, but a split second later the door closed and vanished completely. Jeremy waved his hands through the air where it had been but felt nothing.

Then the ground stopped shaking. He turned and looked up. A huge, menacing form loomed over him, with mighty jaws filled with countless razorlike teeth. As the teeth descended toward him, Jeremy coldly realized that Stephen had been right: Tyrannosaurus Rex really was blue.

THE WILL OF
WHEEZINGLE

MR. KRANTZ DIED ON A MONDAY. MOLLY SAW THE
ambulance and the crowd of people in front of his house
when she arrived home from school. She spotted her mom
among the people gathered on the sidewalk in front of the
grand old house, with its dark slate roof, its ornately gabled
windows, and its castlelike turrets.

"What's going on?" Molly asked when she reached
her mom.

A pudgy face appeared around her mom's skirt.
Molly's little brother, Travis, was clamped to his mother's
leg and said, "Mr. Krantz croaked."

"Travis!" his mother scolded. She put her arm around
Molly's shoulders and looked to the house, where
paramedics were wheeling out the body covered with a sheet.

"What happened?" Molly asked.

"His housekeeper came this afternoon, like she does
every Monday," her mother said, "and found him collapsed
on the floor. A heart attack, it looks like."

Molly watched the covered gurney rolling down the
sidewalk and tried to picture kindly old Mr. Krantz lying

beneath the sheet. She hadn't known him very well, but she liked him. She would wave and say hello when she saw him outside, which was rare, and once when he had locked himself out of his house she had invited him in out of the rain and kept him company until the locksmith arrived.

Molly found her eyes filling with tears. He was the first person she ever knew who died.

—————

Molly's mom read about the funeral plans in the newspaper and asked Molly if she wanted to go. It was to be held during school, but her mom said that was okay. Molly said yes.

So on Thursday morning they went together to the memorial service. Molly noticed that she was the only child there. She recognized the housekeeper but not any of the other handful of people, who were all old men like Mr. Krantz and spoke to one another in hushed voices.

After that day, Molly remembered Mr. Krantz whenever she passed his house, but otherwise he faded from her thoughts. She didn't think much about him until several weeks later when she received a letter that her mother had to sign for. The envelope bore the name of an attorney, and inside was a letter that said, in very official-looking type, that she had been named in Mr. Krantz's will and was invited to the reading the next week.

"What does this mean?" Molly asked her mother.

"It means that Mr. Krantz remembered your kindness and wanted to give you something to remember him by."

Molly looked at the letter again. "What did he want to give me?"

Her mother studied the letter over Molly's shoulder. "I don't know. We'll have to go to the reading of his will to find out."

—=◆=—

Molly wore her best dress for the reading of the will. When it was almost time, she and her mother walked to Mr. Krantz's house. Molly had never been inside it before. From the look of the elegant old house, she expected lots of antique furniture and paintings. She was surprised to find the entrance hall filled with framed posters advertising magic shows. They all featured a magician called the Wondrous Wheezingle performing amazing feats such as making elephants disappear and locomotives vanish. As Molly studied the posters, she realized that the likeness of Wheezingle, with his arched eyebrows and hooked nose, looked familiar.

"Hey!" she said. "That's Mr. Krantz!"

One of the old men from the memorial service walked over, chuckling. "Yes, his stage name was the Wondrous Wheezingle."

"He was a magician?" Molly asked incredulously.

"Why yes," the man said, smiling in delight. He waved at the other old men from the memorial service, who were also waiting in the entrance hall. "We're all magicians. But Wheezingle was the best of us. Some of his illusions baffled even us."

"Wow!" Molly said. She continued to study the posters, and then she and her mother followed the others through the house to the office where the reading was to take place. On the way, they stopped to marvel at other posters, photographs, and props displayed around the house.

"I had no idea he was a magician," Molly said. "I guess I thought he always just lived here and . . . I don't know . . . did nothing."

"I know what you mean," said her mom, who seemed as surprised as her daughter.

They took their seats in the office when Mr. Krantz's attorney arrived. He said good morning to everyone and then proceeded to read the will. Molly paid strict attention at first, but it was a lot of legal information, and her attention wandered to the newspaper clippings framed on the wall next to her, which told how the Wondrous Wheezingle had astounded the royal court of a European country by making the crown jewels vanish and reappear. But when the attorney reached the part of the will that dictated who received what, Molly's attention snapped back to him.

Mr. Krantz left all of his money to his housekeeper, who broke down in tears when she heard. Each of his fellow magicians received a treasured piece of magical apparatus. The balance of his collection was to go to the Museum of Magic—with one exception.

"To Molly Green," the attorney read, "who was kind when I needed kindness, I leave the wand of the Wondrous Wheezingle and ask only that she follow the instructions that come with it."

That concluded the reading of the will. The old men clustered together to discuss the various items they had been bequeathed, and the housekeeper fled the room, presumably to find a washroom to compose herself. The attorney stepped around the desk, made his way to Molly, and presented her with a flat, black case like the kind jewelry comes in, but over a foot long.

"There's a note on its use inside," he said. He seemed as if he were going to say more, but the old men stole him away with questions regarding their own inheritances.

Molly opened the case and gazed at the wand, which was glossy blacklike glass and carved with arcane symbols. She unfolded the small piece of parchment tucked inside and read:

> To vanish—tap once; "Zoozaz." To return—wave wand; "Zazooz." Warning: Do not, under any circumstances, use the wand on a human being.

"Wow!" her mother said, admiring the wand. "It's very pretty, isn't it?"

Molly nodded but didn't look at her mother. She was a little disappointed. She had been hoping for money that she could spend that afternoon at the mall. The wand was pretty, in a museumy sort of way, but so what? What was she supposed to do with it? She couldn't wear it like jewelry, and she'd look stupid carrying a wand around any time except at Halloween.

"I wonder how much it's worth," Molly wondered aloud.

"Molly!" her mother said sharply. "Mr. Krantz left it to you because he wanted you to have it, not so you could sell it."

"I know, I know. I wasn't going to sell it. I was just wondering, is all."

But if someone in the room offered her $20 for it, she wasn't sure she would say no.

It was several nights later that Molly took the wand off her dresser and actually took it out of the case. It was heavier than she had expected, making her think it had been carved from some sort of black stone rather than glass. The wand fit comfortably in her hand, and she laughed at herself in her vanity mirror as she waved it theatrically through the air.

"Abracadabra!" she said as she tapped the Raggedy Ann doll on the vanity. The doll stared back at her.

She waved the wand and pointed it at her bed. "Hocus pocus!"

She spied the stuffed duck, Mr. Quackers, on her dresser, but she couldn't think of any other magic words from movies or TV. She remembered the slip of paper in the wand's case and read the odd words written in quotation marks.

She tapped Mr. Quackers and said, "Zoozaz!"

The duck disappeared.

Molly blinked at where the duck had been and then looked wildly around, as if it might have fallen on the floor when she blinked. But it was nowhere to be found. She dove back to the wand's case and again consulted the slip of paper.

"To return—wave wand; 'Zazooz.' "

Molly took a deep breath. She waved the wand grandly through the air and said, "Zazooz."

Mr. Quackers reappeared right in front of her.

Molly squealed in excitement. She rushed to Raggedy Ann. "Zoozaz!" The doll vanished. She ran over to her bed. "Zazooz!" The doll reappeared on her pillow.

"This is so cool!" she said.

She spent another 15 minutes making things vanish and reappear—jewelry, clothes, even her dresser and her bed. She recalled the posters in Mr. Krantz's house that advertised his making elephants and trains disappear, and her mind boggled at the possibilities.

———❖———

Molly took the wand with her to school the next day. Before she left home, she made her book bag and lunch disappear. When she got to school, she made them reappear. It was wonderful!

At lunch, she told her friend Veronica that she had learned a magic trick and wanted to show it to her. Veronica was so impressed by Molly's disappearing brownie trick that she called over some other kids, and by the end of the lunch period Molly was making whole trays of food disappear and reappear for everyone in the lunchroom. Even the teachers in the cafeteria applauded and told her how good she was.

For the rest of the day, Molly was the center of attention. Everyone—even Francine Turner, the most popular girl in school—wanted her to make things disappear. After Molly had worked her magic on Francine's history book, the girl invited Molly to come to her birthday party on Saturday.

Molly was in heaven, and things only got better. After school, she and Veronica were at the mall, and she discovered another use for the wand. They were trying on outfits in a clothing store, and Molly found a skirt she adored. It would be absolutely *perfect* with her pink blouse and just the thing to wear to Francine's birthday party, but she didn't have enough money to buy it. So when the racks of clothing blocked her from view, she removed the wand from her purse and made the skirt disappear.

When she got home later that evening, she made the skirt reappear. She hugged it to her chest and rolled on her bed. Thanks to the wand of the Wondrous Wheezingle, she was going to have everything she ever wanted.

⇒◆⇐

Recalling the poster advertising Wheezingle's making an elephant disappear, Molly made Francine's Saint Bernard vanish and was the hit of the party on Saturday. After that, Molly's popularity soared. Everyone wanted her to come to their birthday parties or just to come over and hang out—and make things disappear.

Soon she was spending almost all of her time out. At first her mother seemed pleased with her daughter's popularity. Then she became concerned about how suddenly Molly's life had changed. She asked several times how Molly made items disappear, but Molly always answered, "Magic" or "A good magician never reveals her secrets."

Her mom noticed the new clothes, CDs, and other items Molly had been acquiring thanks to the wand. Molly explained them away by saying that they were gifts for performing at parties or that she bought them with money she had made performing. Molly felt her mother watching her with concern whenever she left the house, but as long as Molly kept up her grades, there didn't seem to be a problem.

⇒◆⇐

The problem came one evening when Molly was supposed to meet friends at the mall. Francine's cousin Brent, who went to a different school, was going to be there, and Francine had told Molly that Brent liked her. Molly spent an hour getting dressed so she would look just right, but when she was finally ready her mother knocked on her bedroom door.

"Molly, there's an emergency at my office, and I have to go in for a few hours," her mother said, leaning into the bedroom. "I need you to stay here and keep an eye on Travis."

Molly's jaw dropped at the unfairness of the situation. "I can't!" she said. "I have plans."

"I'm sorry, but you're going to have to cancel them."

Molly huffed crossly. "Why can't you just take him with you?"

"Because there's no place for him there, and I'll be too busy to watch him."

"Well, what about Dad?" Molly asked. "He'll be home soon."

Her mother shook her head. "His car is in the shop. I'm supposed to pick him up at work, and he's going to be stuck there until I finish up at the office. Sorry, Molly, but you're it. I'll leave money in the kitchen so you can order a pizza for dinner. See you in a few hours."

After her mother left, Molly threw herself on the bed. This was horrible! Francine had told Brent that Molly would be there. Now he would think that she had stood him up and couldn't care less about him.

The bedroom door opened, and Travis came in, waving the money their mother had left for pizza. "Call! Call! Call!" he chanted as he paraded around the room.

Molly glared at him. "I ought to make you disappear," she muttered. Thinking about what she had just said, she sat up. Maybe that wasn't such a bad idea. She remembered the warning that had come with the magic wand—not to use it on human beings—but what was the big deal? She had used it on Francine's Saint Bernard with no problem.

Molly reached for her purse on the nightstand and drew forth the magic wand.

"Come here, Travis," she said sweetly. "I want to show you a trick."

———◆———

Things went extremely well at the mall. Molly met Brent and the others, and then just the two of them went to the food court for ice cream. They exchanged phone numbers and he absolutely promised he would call her later that night. Molly couldn't wait.

When she arrived home again, she was amazed at how much time had passed. She had no sooner gotten in the door than her mom and dad pulled up outside. Molly ran for her room and the magic wand. She snatched it up from where she had left it on the bed.

With a wave of the wand, she said, "Zazooz!"

Nothing happened.

A cold fear gripped Molly as once again she recalled the warning not to use the wand on human beings. She heard the front door open as she waved the wand again.

"Zazooz!"

Still Travis did not appear. Had too much time passed? She had made things disappear for longer periods of time—overnight even—and had had no problem making them reappear. She had never before had to say the magic word more than once.

"Zazooz!"

She heard her parents coming up the stairs.

"Molly! Travis!" her mom called. "We're home." Her footsteps headed in the direction of Molly's room.

"Zazooz, zazooz, zazooz!" Molly chanted desperately, closing her eyes and concentrating. What was she going to tell her parents? How was she going to explain Travis's absence?

"What are you two up to in here?" her mother asked.

Molly opened her eyes and found Travis standing in front of her. She expelled a huge sigh of relief.

"Nothing, Mom," she said. "Just playing."

She smiled at Travis, but oddly he didn't smile back. Travis always smiled. He was the most annoyingly happy kid on the planet. But he didn't smile now. He looked at Molly solemnly and narrowed his eyes.

"Travis?" his mother questioned.

He looked over his shoulder at her. Molly could see his expression change. He smiled at his mother, but when he looked back at Molly the smile disappeared once again.

"Come on, Travis," his mother said. "It's time for you to go to bed."

Reluctantly, it seemed to Molly, he turned away and ambled over to his mother. Smiling again, he took her hand and followed her toward his own room. Molly collapsed on her bed, more relieved than she had ever been in her life. Her heart was beating a million times a minute, but she had pulled it off. She had gotten what she wanted, and everything had turned out all right.

Or so she thought.

It was after midnight when the lights came on in her room, waking her. She blinked, raising a hand to shield her eyes against the sudden brightness. Just inside her closed door stood Travis. Only he was different. He regarded her with the same solemn look he had worn earlier. Suddenly, it struck Molly what was so wrong. The look on his face was *not* the expression of a toddler. It was the expression of someone older—much older.

"Travis," she asked, "what's wrong?"

He stepped closer to the bed, and when he spoke it was in a hollow, whispery voice that did not belong to Travis.

"I am not your brother," he said. "He is still in the Disappearing Place."

Chills shot through Molly. This is a dream, she thought, but she knew it wasn't. Everything was far too real.

"I am Zoozaz, Lord of the Disappearing Place. You have violated the rule of the wand, so your brother shall remain in my domain."

"No," Molly breathed.

"The rule of the wand has been broken. It must be so."

"Please," she begged. "You can't."

"There is only one alternative," Zoozaz told her. "If you so choose, you may take your brother's place in the Disappearing Place."

Molly started to tremble. Travis was a pest sometimes, but she did love him. Still, was she willing to trade places with him? And what would she tell her parents if she didn't? Molly started to cry.

"What is it like there?" she asked.

"The Disappearing Place has many outstanding qualities," Zoozaz told her. "There is no war there, and no crime. There is no sickness, no hunger, no evil. There you can do anything you want to do."

That didn't sound too bad, Molly thought. And she would never be able to face her parents with Travis gone, she realized guiltily.

"Okay," she said. "I'll trade places with Travis."

"So shall it be," Zoozaz responded.

He waved a hand, and everything went completely black. Molly waited for a few seconds, wondering how long it would take to get to the Disappearing Place. She had thought it would work instantly, like the wand.

Then with a horrible certainty she realized that it *had.*

There was no war or crime or evil because there was *nothing* in the Disappearing Place—no light, no sounds, nothing. As Zoozaz had said, she was free to do anything she wanted, but there was nothing for her to do. And, she realized, her horror growing out of control, she had eternity to spend doing it.

THE MAD
REVEREND JENKS

⸻

ARE WE THERE YET?" ROBBY ASKED FOR THE FIFTH time in as many miles.

Karen turned from the sun setting over the endless cornfields outside her window and glared at her little brother. After eight hours in the minivan, she had had about as much of his whining as she could stand.

"Almost, sweetheart," their mother said from behind the steering wheel.

"Only a few more miles," their father said from the passenger seat, where he studied a road atlas and the realtor's faxed instructions. "I think," he added in a mumble, "Otis isn't even on this map."

Otis. What a stupid, stupid name for a town, Karen thought. It made her think of toothless old men in overalls, scratching themselves. When it came time to name this place, all the good names must already have been taken.

And they were going to live there. Maybe Columbus hadn't been the biggest city in the world, but Karen had liked living there. She had her friends and the skating rink and the mall. There were things to do there. What could you do in a place called Otis? Spit watermelon seeds at the dog and watch the corn grow? Her mom said she would make friends there too, but Karen had her doubts.

"Are we there yet?" Robby asked.

Karen gripped the armrest as the urge to turn and choke her little brother swelled within her. But then, as she looked down the seemingly endless road that divided the sea of corn, something distracted her. A dark figure was walking, on her side of the car, in the same direction they were traveling. Her father must have noticed it too.

"We can ask this person how far we are from Otis," he suggested.

As they drove nearer, Karen saw that the figure was a man, tall and straight, dressed in grim black. Even his shoes and the wide-brimmed hat on his head were black. The only other color to him was his hair, which flowed to his shoulders as red as fire. He strode down the side of the road so deliberately that he seemed under the weight of some great purpose.

The man didn't even look around at them until the minivan had almost reached him and Karen's mother had begun to slow down. When he glanced back over his shoulder, Karen gasped. The man didn't seem all that old, but his face was gaunt and angular, his worn, reddish skin pulled tight over sharp cheekbones and a high forehead. His nose was sharp, and his lips stretched tight in grim determination. But his most striking feature was his eyes, which were black and burned with an intensity that pushed Karen back in her seat.

The minivan sped up again, swerving widely around the man. No one spoke for several seconds. Then Karen's mom looked nervously back at them, and then at her husband. "I'm sure we're almost there," she said.

———⊰◆⊱———

She turned out to be right. After another mile or so they came within sight of Otis. It was about what Karen had expected—one main street with a small grocery store, the volunteer fire department, a farm-equipment dealer, a feed store, and a gas station with a small diner.

"We're going to need to ask for directions," Karen's father said as he studied the hand-drawn map the real estate agent had faxed him. "Some of these streets aren't labeled."

Karen's mom turned into the diner's parking lot. "This diner looks good," she said. "We can get directions and something to eat."

They all piled out of the minivan and, stretching and groaning, made their way into the diner. A round face topped by thick gray curls peeked out through the window that looked into the kitchen.

"Why, hello!" the woman called. She came bustling through the kitchen doors, removing a white apron from over her light blue dress. "I'm Mabel. Four for dinner?"

Karen's dad said yes, and Mabel seated them in a booth. They were the only diners in the place. She handed out menus and told them about the special for the evening— meatloaf with mashed potatoes.

They all ordered, and then Mabel disappeared for 20 minutes, though they could hear her going about her business in the kitchen. When she returned she served up their orders piping hot.

"You folks passing through Otis?" she asked as she distributed the plates. To Karen the meals looked and smelled heavenly.

Her father explained about his new job and that they were on their way to the house they would be renting. While on the subject, he pulled out his faxed map, and Mabel helpfully filled in the missing street names for him.

"You're going to love the place," she said. "My niece lives a few houses down from you. You have some very nice neighbors."

"Not like that creepy guy we saw, I hope," Robby said around a mouthful of hamburger. He shivered melodramatically.

Their parents laughed, but Mabel looked concerned. "What creepy guy would that be?"

"Oh, just some gentleman we saw outside of town," her father said.

Mabel looked out the front window of the diner with alarm. "Dressed all in black," she said. It wasn't a question. "With red hair like fire and a look of relentless determination on his face."

"Yes," Karen's father said, puzzled. "You know him?"

Mabel looked at them again, all traces of humor gone from her face. "Everyone around here knows him. You saw the ghost of the mad Reverend Jenks."

Karen, caught taking a sip of her soda, almost choked.

Her mother gave Mabel the same gentle smile she gave Robby when he woke up in the middle of the night convinced monsters were lurking in his closet. "He didn't look much like a ghost," she said. "He looked pretty real to me."

Mabel nodded. "He always does, this time of the day. He only appears at dusk, walking along Church Hill Road as if on a mission for a higher power. Or a lower one."

"Well, it sounds like someone playing a joke to me," Karen's mother said. "Has this been going on very long?"

"Nearly a hundred years," Mabel assured them. "Last century, the church used to be on a hill a few miles outside of town. The Reverend Jenks came after the previous reverend passed away. They say when he preached his fiery sermons the stained-glass windows trembled in their frames. Folks who used to show up in church only every so often started coming every Sunday— not just because he was such a powerful speaker, but because they were afraid not to, afraid the Reverend Jenks would come to see them and turn his wrathful attention on them."

"Is that why they called him the *mad* Reverend Jenks?" Robby asked. "Because he always looked so angry?"

"Oh, no," Mabel told him. "Not mad as in *angry*— mad as in *crazy*. And they didn't start calling him that until after . . . well, perhaps it's not a fit topic for the dinner table."

Karen's mother looked relieved, but Robby cried, "No, how come they called him that?"

Karen found herself nodding, wanting to hear the rest of the story despite the goose bumps that had risen on her skin.

Her father, with an amused smile, said, "Go on. You can't stop now."

Mabel took another look outside, where the sun had set almost completely. Only its last fiery edge showed through the growing darkness.

"The Reverend had been here almost a year when it happened. After services on Sundays, he taught the Sunday school class. His services were running the entire morning and into the afternoon by then, and his Sunday school classes weren't much shorter. The kids, being kids, were not suited to sitting still as long as their parents. This particular Sunday, the students were talking and fidgeting, and the Reverend exploded with ire. To punish them, he said, he would show them what it would be like in hell, and he stoked the stoves in the church until they glowed red. The heat built up in the church and became stifling. The children sweated and swooned while the Reverend walked among them, preaching with burning passion.

"But the fires in the stoves were too much for their chimneys and set the roof of the church on fire. The Reverend always kept the doors locked during Sunday school so that none of the kids could sneak out, and . . . well, a few escaped out the windows, but most perished in the fire, including the Reverend himself. Now to this day they say that each evening, at dusk, he walks Church Hill Road, looking for the children who escaped."

They had all stopped eating and now watched Mabel, frozen. Then the bell attached to the door rang as several men came into the diner. Karen and her family started at the unexpected sound. Then Robby started to giggle, and they all smiled.

"Excuse me," Mabel said as she went to seat the new diners. "Enjoy your meals."

"Well," Karen's father said after Mabel was gone. "That was quite a story."

Her mother looked at Karen. "And you thought it was going to be boring here."

—————✦—————

After dinner they headed back out of town the way they had come and turned at the first road. They found their new house a few minutes afterward and had fun exploring it with flashlights. That first night the power had not even been turned on, so they had to camp on the floor by the light of a battery-powered lantern. Robby wanted to tell ghost stories, but their mother said they had had enough ghost stories for one day, which reminded Karen of the mad Reverend Jenks and the man they had seen on the road. She didn't believe in ghosts and didn't think they were one and the same, but the man's appearance on the road was quite a coincidence. That night she had a difficult time going to sleep, but whether it was because of the uncomfortable floor or the memory of the man's intense gaze she wasn't sure.

The next morning the moving van arrived with the rest of their belongings. Many busy days followed as they unpacked and settled into their new house. Her father started his new job, which left the rest of the work to Karen, Robby, and their mother. About 20 miles away was a good-size town, where they made frequent trips for food, cleaning supplies, and odds and ends they needed for their new house. Karen was delighted to find a mall there even bigger than the one in Columbus.

They still were not finished unpacking by the time school started. Karen didn't sleep much the night before her first day, but she came home the next afternoon excited and talking a mile a minute, having made a bunch of new friends.

Though she had been afraid that there would be nothing to do after they moved, Karen found herself extremely busy with her new house and new friends—so busy, in fact, that she forgot all about the story of the mad Reverend Jenks and the sinister figure striding down the side of the road. After that first day, it was several weeks until she recalled the story.

One thing she liked about Otis was that the traffic on the roads was nothing compared to traffic in the city. She could ride her bike all over the place without constantly having to worry about cars all around her.

One Saturday, she rode her bike to her friend Jennifer's house. It was several miles away, but the weather was pleasant and Karen loved to ride. She spent most of the day there, swimming in Jennifer's pool and watching videos with their other friends. Before she knew it, the sun had started its slow descent in the western sky, and she had to head home. As she set off down Jennifer's long gravel driveway, Mrs. Montgomery, who had come to pick up her daughter Mary, another of Karen's friends, pulled alongside her and offered to drive her home.

"No, thank you," Karen said. "I like to ride my bike."

"But," Mrs. Montgomery said, casting a nervous look to the west, "the sun is setting. It's almost dusk."

"That's okay," Karen said. "It won't take me very long to get home, and my bike has a light and reflectors if it gets too dark."

Reluctantly, it seemed, Mrs. Montgomery gave up and drove away. Karen pumped the pedals of her bike and turned onto Church Hill Road. With no traffic in sight, she could drift to the center of the lane, pedaling hard so that she swiftly built up speed and the wind sang through her hair. The sun was sinking below the horizon, painting the sky in gorgeous oranges and pinks as darkness started to settle. It was such a great feeling to be cruising along the open road at the end of such a beautiful day.

Karen glanced over her shoulder to make sure no cars were coming. The road was empty of traffic, but far behind her a tiny, dark figure was walking down the side of the road.

For the first time in weeks, she thought of the mad Reverend Jenks and the scary man they had seen on this very road that first night in Otis. Though a shiver ran through her, she didn't really believe that the figure could be the Reverend Jenks. Still, she pedaled harder.

After another minute, she glanced back, feeling confident that the tiny figure would now be completely out of sight. Instead, she was shocked to find that the figure had *grown*. Now, instead of only a black speck in the distance, she could make out the man in black with arms and legs moving as he strode purposefully down the side of the road.

Karen faced forward once again redoubling her efforts. Her legs pumped so fiercely that she could feel her muscles straining to the breaking point. She breathed hard with the rhythm of her pedaling, and sweat trickled down her face.

After another minute, she glanced back again, hoping the figure would be gone—or at least farther away. With mounting horror she saw that yet again the figure had grown. She could make out the fiery red of his hair. And was it her imagination, or could she see the bottomless fury that raged in his eyes?

Her bike struck a stone in the roadway, and she snapped her head around to keep her bike upright. Her stomach felt as if it had been pumped full of cold air as she fought to regain her balance. If she crashed and injured herself or damaged her bike . . . well, she didn't want to think about what might happen.

She managed to keep going and once again built up her speed as high as she could. Her muscles were burning with fatigue, but she didn't even think about letting up. It was only another mile or so to her turnoff, and less than that from there to her house. She only had to hang on a little while longer.

She knew it would be best not to look back again, to avoid hitting any more stones or a pothole. But the thought of him back there, gaining on her, made the skin on her back prickle as if at any moment she might feel his fingers touch her there. She had to look back.

She turned her head and scanned the roadway behind her. To her immense relief, she no longer saw any sign of the man following her. She studied the road behind her carefully to make sure, and she was certain: The man was gone.

As she turned back around, her relief turned to terror. There, right in her path, not 10 feet away, stood the mad Reverend Jenks in all his wrath and fury. She tugged at the handlebars to swerve around him, but he reached out like lightning and snatched her off her bike. It crashed onto the asphalt as he locked her under one steely arm and resumed walking. But instead of following the road now, he struck off into the grass, toward the top of the barren hill nearby.

Karen screamed for help. She thrashed and grabbed at the arm that held her, but it was like a band of iron. The Reverend seemed more like a machine than a man as he tirelessly bore her across the field. And as he walked, he began to speak. Though she could not make out his words clearly, they struck like thunderbolts and rang in her ears as if the sky were splitting open. Everyone in Otis must have heard them, she felt sure, but as they climbed the hill she looked back at the road. It was empty, merely a darker stripe in the growing gloom.

"No!" Karen cried out, still trying to squirm free, but she could not even hear herself over the Reverend's thunderous words.

Then, as she struggled and twisted in his grip, she smelled a familiar odor: smoke. She stretched her neck to glance up the hill, and there she saw their ultimate destination. On the bare hilltop, a burning fire outlined a steepled building against the darkness of the sky. The Reverend did not slow in his march toward its doors.

Karen screamed mindlessly and pounded against the Reverend's body, but it was like striking a statue. He paid no attention to her as he continued to preach his earth-shaking sermon. Smoke twisted through the air and embraced them. Karen coughed and shielded her eyes as the blinding church of fire loomed before them. Still the Reverend did not hesitate but mounted the steps of flame. It was impossible; being made of fire, they should not have borne his weight, but they did.

Karen felt the singe of the heat on her skin as they approached the doorway leading into the inferno, and now she was finally able to hear something over the Reverend's deafening words. From within the church came a horrifying chorus of screams, the tormented shrieks of the children locked inside.

Karen's screams joined theirs as she was carried into the heart of that evil inferno by her dark captor, the mad Reverend Jenks.

THE LITTLE PEOPLE

SEVERAL MOUTH-WATERING AROMAS SWIRLED around the kitchen: roasting turkey, mashed potatoes, candied yams, homemade cranberry sauce, fresh rolls, buttered corn, and pumpkin pie. Elliot followed his mother into the kitchen, shucking his jacket. He sniffed deeply, savoring the delicious mix of aromas.

"Everything smells great, Grandma," he said by way of greeting.

"Why, thank you, Elliot," she replied. She turned away from the stove, a pig-puppet oven mitt on one hand and a large spoon gripped in the other. Her long apron said "My Kitchen—My Rules!"

"Wow," Elliot's mother said as she surveyed the food filling the counters, the table, and even the window sills. "Mom, you really didn't have to go to all this trouble just for us."

Grandma raised the pig-puppet oven mitt and made it say "Nonsense!"

Elliot laughed.

"I don't get to see my only daughter and my only grandson very often," Grandma said. "I wanted dinner to be special." She made a show of looking behind them. "Didn't Joe come with you?"

Before they could answer, the TV roared to life in the living room, and the sound of a football game rose until it sounded as if the players and the stadium full of screaming fans were in the next room.

Elliot's mom looked sorry, but Grandma just smiled and checked on the pots simmering on the range. Elliot scowled, wishing that Grandma had been right and Joe had not come with them. His mom's boyfriend was loud and obnoxious and very rude—as he had demonstrated by not even coming into the kitchen to say hi to Grandma before planting himself in front of the TV. Elliot knew that Grandma didn't like Joe either, but she seemed determined not to let him ruin their visit, so Elliot decided he wouldn't either.

"Is there anything we can do to help?" Elliot's mother asked as she glanced around the room.

"Just have a seat," Grandma told her, "and keep me company. I want to hear all about what's going on in your lives."

Elliot and his mom sat at the kitchen table, and his mom started to tell Grandma that they were looking for a new apartment to share with Joe.

"It'll be a lot less expensive with him helping out with the rent and utilities," his mother said, as if trying to convince both Grandma and herself that it was a good idea.

"Huh," Grandma said, concentrating on her cooking. Then she turned and grinned at Elliot. "I understand you're helping out now too. Have a job, do you?"

Elliot nodded. "I deliver the bargain shopper on Wednesdays," he said. "I kind of wish it came out more than once a week so I could make more money, but it *is* a lot of work. Those newspapers are heavy."

A sudden shout from the living room startled all of them: "Holly, honey—bring me a beer, would you?"

Elliot's mom looked at Grandma. "Do you happen to have any?"

"Only a few bottles," she said disapprovingly, "so tell him to pace himself. It's in the refrigerator."

Elliot's mom opened a bottle and took it out to Joe. *He couldn't even get up to get his own beer,* Elliot thought. He didn't even know why Joe had come. All Joe did was complain about having to waste his Thanksgiving at Grandma's, watching her "dinky little TV set." As if he had anything better to do. If they weren't here, he would be lying on the couch at Elliot and his mom's apartment, watching their ancient black-and-white set. He just seemed to like to complain and put down everything.

"So," Grandma said to Elliot, "what are you doing with all the money you're making?"

Elliot perked up. "Mom and I have this bank that looks like a giant crayon. I put all my money in it, and Mom puts in all her loose change. We call it our TV Fund. When they have all the big sales around Christmas, we're going to take all the money and buy the biggest TV we can get."

Then Elliot's mom came back into the room and rejoined them. She told Grandma about her job and their neighbors in their apartment building, and then Elliot told her about how he had taught his dog, Charlie, to roll over.

Grandma moved around the kitchen, not quickly but steadily, doing several things at once. At one point she looked around the kitchen and said, "I've forgotten the green beans."

Elliot's mom said, "That's okay. You've got plenty of other food."

Grandma shook her head. "I know green beans are Elliot's favorite. I grew a bunch in my garden this year and canned them. I've got a dozen or so jars in the basement. I was looking forward to his trying them. I'll just run down and get a jar. It'll only take a few minutes to warm them up."

But after she had taken one step toward the basement door, the oven timer went off. She stopped and glanced back at the stove uncertainly.

Elliot jumped out of his chair, glad to have an opportunity to help. "That's okay, Grandma. I'll get the green beans."

"No, that's not necessary—" she started to say.

But Elliot reached the basement door before she could finish. He flipped on the lights and started down the wooden stairs. The air was cool and still, though he thought he heard some faint skittering sounds. As he reached the bottom of the stairs, he realized he had never been in the basement before. It was bigger than he had expected. The two bare light bulbs provided only a little light, leaving most of the basement shrouded in shadows. Old boxes and a long workbench filled most of it, and at the far end of the single room he saw the shelves. The light gleamed dully off dusty glass jars filled with colorful, neatly sorted foods: green beans, corn, pickles, peaches, and tomatoes. But before Elliot could make his way toward them, Grandma started down the steps behind him.

"Quite a mess, isn't it?" she said cheerfully. She carried something wrapped in aluminum foil. "Before we do anything else down here, we have to take care of the Little People."

"The who?" Elliot asked.

"The Little People," she repeated, leading Elliot a few paces from the bottom of the stairs to where an aluminum pie pan rested on the floor. "They live here in the basement. Oh, I've never seen them, but I've heard them a few times. I always make sure to bring them something to eat when I come down here, just to stay on their good side."

She unwrapped the aluminum foil and revealed a steaming drumstick from the turkey she had spent all day preparing. "Usually I just give them some day-old bread or some stale cookies," she said as she placed the drumstick in the pie pan, "but it's Thanksgiving. They should have something special too."

As she headed toward the end of the basement to get the green beans, Elliot followed sadly. He loved his grandmother very much, and when his mother had expressed worry about her living in this house all alone, Elliot had always stood up for her. But he didn't think he would be able to do that anymore, because now he knew for sure that Grandma was crazy.

⋙◆⋘

Elliot didn't have long to worry about his grandmother's sanity. Less than a week after they had all enjoyed a delicious Thanksgiving feast together, Elliot and his mother received the horrible news: Grandma had died.

At first Elliot imagined all kinds of things—that her delusions about the Little People had somehow been responsible for her death—but the truth turned out to be much more mundane. She had simply tripped on her robe one morning and fallen down the stairs from the second floor. It had all been over very quickly, and for that, at least, everyone was grateful.

Several weeks after they had received the news, Elliot's mom came to his room one night before bedtime and asked him a question that took him by surprise.

"How would you like to live in Grandma's house?"

Elliot had to think about it. It would be sort of strange, knowing that Grandma had died there, but it was a nice house and held many happy memories.

"Yeah," he said. "Grandma would have liked that."

"I do too," she said.

Elliot was happy at the thought until he started to wonder: *Would Joe be moving in with them?*

⸻⬦⸻

The answer to that question, as Elliot had dreaded, turned out to be yes. One Saturday, Joe came with a borrowed pickup truck and they started to move all their belongings out of the apartment and into Grandma's house. It was a frantic day, with many trips back and forth using the pickup and his mom's car. On the trip to his grandmother's house, after Elliot had been in the backyard playing with Charlie, he came inside to find Joe looking through a box of his mother's things.

Joe was of average height but broad, with arms that bulged through the sleeves of his black T-shirt and a rounded gut that did the same. His black hair was short, shaved up the back of his neck, and his nose had a small kink in it— from his boxing days, he said. He worked in a garage

88

repairing cars and never seemed to get all the grease off his hands. Elliot watched him putting his blunt, grease-blackened fingers on his mom's clothes and grew angry.

"What are you doing?" Elliot demanded. "Where's Mom?"

Joe's head snapped up at the sound, but then a sly smile came over his face. "Just checking to see where this box goes, Ellie," he said.

Elliot hated it when he called him that. Joe wouldn't do it when Elliot's mother was around, but when she wasn't he said Elliot acted like a girl and should have a girl's name.

Joe hoisted the box in his burly arms and started toward Elliot. The size of the box made it impossible for him to see what was right in front of him. Elliot had to step aside to avoid getting run over. He followed Joe into the kitchen and toward the stairs up to the second floor, to keep an eye on him.

Charlie, thirsty after playing outside with Elliot, was getting a drink out of his bowl. The dog was a mutt, with the golden hair of a collie and patches of white. His barrel-shaped body was low to the ground, but he had bright, happy eyes and boundless energy.

Because of the box, Joe didn't see the dog and tripped over him. He crashed down and landed on the box, half flattening it. Charlie skittered away. Joe pushed himself up, cursing at the dog.

"It's not his fault," Elliot said. "He didn't do anything."

Joe reached out and hooked a finger through the dog's collar. Then he dragged Charlie across the kitchen floor to the basement door. Elliot chased after them, trying to get Charlie away from Joe.

"Leave him alone!" Elliot cried.

Joe opened the basement door and shoved Charlie through.

"He's in the way," Joe said. "And, come to think of it, so are you, Ellie."

He grabbed Elliot by the arm and spun him through the doorway into the darkness. Elliot tripped down the first few stairs but then managed to grab hold of the railing. He hung onto it as he slid the rest of the way down the stairs to the cold concrete floor at the bottom. The door above closed, and he heard the rattle of the lock being turned.

"Charlie," he whispered in the darkness, "are you okay?"

Charlie's snout nudged him from the side, and he felt the dog's warm breath on his arm. The dog seemed fine, and aside from a scrape on his ankle, so did Elliot. He pushed himself to his feet, trying to get his bearings. A bright slice of light shone beneath the door at the top of the steps, and he could make out the stairs and the workbench by this dim illumination. He also saw the gleam of the aluminum pie pan on the floor. That made him remember the last day he had seen his grandmother, when he was worried about her going crazy, and he realized how much he missed her.

He dug through his pockets and came up with half a candy bar he had been saving for later. Stepping carefully through the darkness, he made his way to the pie pan and placed the candy bar in it. Charlie sniffed at it.

"No, Charlie," he said, pulling the dog away. "That's for the Little People."

But it wasn't really. He put the candy bar there more as a fond tribute to Grandma and her eccentricities than for any small inhabitants of the basement. He didn't really believe in the Little People. Not yet.

Elliot spent the next hour in the basement. When his mother returned, she let him out. Joe claimed that he didn't know Elliot was down there, that he thought Elliot had gone with his mother.

"He must have locked himself in," he said.

Elliot was used to Joe's lies and didn't bother trying to argue. He was too absorbed with thinking about something strange he had observed. When his mother had opened the basement door and turned on the lights, the pie pan in which he had placed the candy bar was empty. *Charlie might have gotten it,* he thought, but he was pretty sure that Charlie had stayed with him as he explored the basement in the dark and found a comfortable place to await his mom's return, on an old sofa hidden among the boxes.

After that day, Elliot spent a lot of time in the basement—it was a good place to get away from Joe. He moved the old boxes around until they completely enclosed the sofa, except for a secret entrance that only he and Charlie were small enough to slip through. He hid a flashlight and snacks and comic books down there, and it was their safe haven. And whenever he went down, he always left something in the pie pan for the Little People.

He still didn't truly believe in them, but after the disappearing candy bar he was not so sure. Sometimes, from within his fort built around the old sofa, he heard scuffling and skittering sounds in the basement, and he started to suspect that he was just feeding mice or rats. But leaving the food and following his grandmother's ritual made him feel closer to her, like caring for her favorite plant to keep her alive in his memory.

It took something extraordinary for him to *really* start believing in the Little People.

—————◆—————

Elliot's mom had run out to the grocery store. Joe had been complaining about being out of beer, so Elliot thought that Joe had gone with her. But when Elliot walked into the living room he found out how wrong he was. There was Joe, having removed the top from the crayon bank, sifting through the money Elliot and his mother had been saving for their new TV. Joe had removed a small stack of bills, which he stuffed into one of his pockets.

Elliot started to back quietly out of the room. He would tell his mom about this, and she would see what a worthless sleaze Joe was and make him leave. But in the meantime he didn't want Joe to know that he had seen him. So when he bumped the end table, making the lamp wobble crazily, his insides seemed to freeze like ice.

Joe spun around, and his eyes narrowed.

"Ellie," he said in a low, dangerous voice. "Didn't your mom ever tell you it's not nice to spy on people?"

Joe pushed the top back on the crayon bank and started to walk slowly toward Elliot. This and the deadly serious look in Joe's eyes scared Elliot more than his fits of rage. Elliot turned and ran from the room into the kitchen. The house shook as Joe thundered after him.

Elliot looked wildly around the kitchen, trying to make up his mind which way to go. He would never get the locks and chains undone in time to make it out the back door. That left a choice between upstairs and the basement—an easy decision. He ran for the basement door and the refuge of his fort.

"Come back here, Ellie!" Joe bellowed.

Elliot charged down the basement steps without bothering with the lights. By now, he was used to moving around down there with the lights off. He reached the bottom of the steps and dodged out of the light streaming down from above just as Joe's shadow eclipsed it.

"Get up here right now!" Joe roared. "If you make me come down there, you're not going to live to regret it!"

Elliot stayed crouched by a pile of boxes, frozen in terror. He heard Joe flick the light switch at the top of the stairs, but strangely the bare bulbs did not go on. Joe grunted in annoyance and then started to come down the steps.

Elliot desperately wanted to make his way through the secret entrance into the safety of his fort, but he was afraid to move. The smallest sound would tell Joe exactly where he was.

"Come on out, Ellie," Joe whispered menacingly when he reached the bottom of the stairs.

Then the door at the top of the stairs swung closed. The darkness in the basement was complete. Joe swore and then started to move around the basement, kicking and throwing boxes around. Elliot cowered beneath the workbench away from the noise. He looked fearfully out into the darkness for some warning of Joe's approach, but what he saw instead shocked him so much he stopped breathing. He saw eyes. Dozens of pairs of tiny glowing eyes no more than a foot above the floor. They stole through the darkness toward the sounds of Joe's fury.

"Get out here!" Joe commanded. But then his shouts of rage changed, rising in pitch to frantic shrieks of pure terror.

Elliot heard him take a few steps up the stairs, but then he screamed again and tumbled back down. His cries and some horrible scuffling sounds continued for a few seconds longer, and then an eerie stillness stole over the basement. Elliot stayed where he was, afraid to even guess what had happened not 10 feet away from him.

Then the basement lights came on, and the biggest shock was how normal everything looked. Elliot saw no sign of Joe. He warily pulled himself out from under the workbench, expecting Joe to jump out from behind a stack of boxes at any moment. However, after looking around for half a minute, he still saw no sign of the man. The only thing out of the ordinary he found was the money Joe had stolen, neatly stacked in the aluminum pie pan.

＝＞◆＜＝

The police didn't look too hard after Joe disappeared. Nobody, it seemed, was too upset—or surprised—that he was gone. Even Elliot's mother seemed more relieved than anything. Everyone assumed he had just decided to pick up and leave the area.

Life seemed a lot better to Elliot after that. He and his mother made a home in Grandma's house, and that Christmas they bought a brand-new 35-inch television set to celebrate. They had enough money in the crayon bank to buy a VCR too.

Elliot spent a lot more of his time in the living room, but he still went down into the basement once every day, to leave something to eat for the Little People. The next day, whatever he had left would always be gone. There was only one exception.

The morning after Joe had disappeared, Elliot went down into the basement and found the cake he had placed in the pie pan still there, and there it remained for the next two days.

Joe, he figured, must have been very filling.